THOMAS TAYLOR
ILLUSTRATED BY TOM BOOTH

WALKER BOOKS

Text and map copyright © 2023 by Thomas Taylor
Illustrations copyright © 2023 by Tom Booth

First US edition 2023

Library of Congress Catalog Card Number 2022908683
ISBN 978-1-5362-2742-0

23 24 25 26 27 28 SHD 10 9 8 7 6 5 4 3 2 1

Printed in Chelsea, MI, USA

This book was typeset in Bell MT.
The illustrations were created digitally.

Walker Books US
a division of
Candlewick Press
99 Dover Street
Somerville, Massachusetts 02144

www.walkerbooksus.com

A JUNIOR LIBRARY GUILD SELECTION

FOR WILLIAM, AIMEE,
EMILY, AND TOBIAS
TT

No seagulls were harmed in the making of this book.

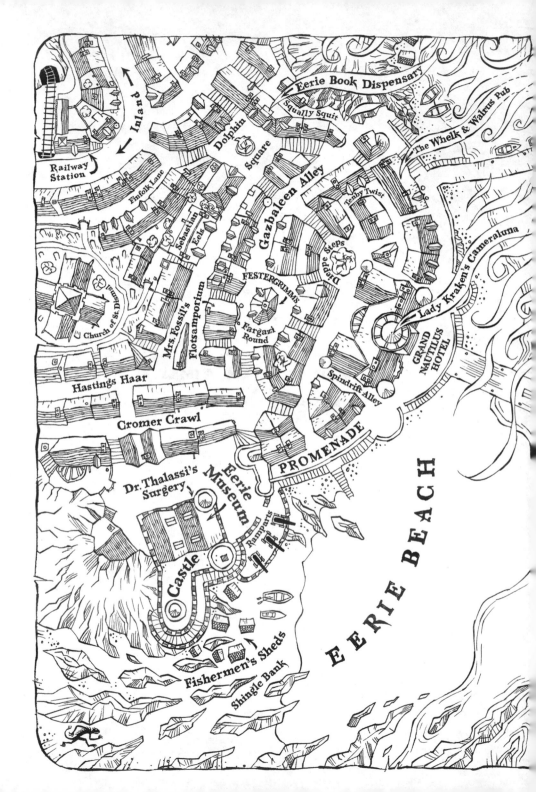

CONTENTS

CHAPTER 1

GHOST TRAIN

··

I t was a cold and blustery day at the wrong end of November when trouble returned to Eerie-on-Sea. Violet spotted it first, of course, but it was I, Herbert Lemon—Lost-and-Founder at the Grand Nautilus Hotel—who had the queasy feeling from the start. The queasy feeling that began when we were sent to meet a surprise hotel guest at the town's tumble-down railway station.

"I didn't even know there *was* a railway station in Eerie-on-Sea," says Vi as we walk through the drafty ticket office and out onto the platform. The rusty old rail track beside it disappears into the gaping mouth of a tunnel hewn long ago into Eerie Rock. "It looks more like the entrance to a ghost train."

"Pah!" Mr. Mollusc replies, with a scowl at the dead leaves that drift along the platform and the one flickering Victorian lamp that illuminates them. The WELCOME TO CHEERIE-ON-SEA station sign creaks like a broken promise—the letters *C* and *H* obscured by a sooty cobweb that no one will wipe away till spring. The wind moans around the wrought-iron columns that hold up the station canopy, and from somewhere there comes a persistent thumping sound that I can't explain.

"No wonder we get so few guests in winter," the hotel manager adds with a shudder.

I glance at my two companions, and my mouth twitches between a smile and a frown. It's not every day I'm out and about with my best friend, Violet Parma, *and* the miserable old manager of the Grand Nautilus Hotel. It's a strange feeling having to deal with both of them at the same time.

"It's not a proper railway service anymore," I explain to Violet. "More of a tourist attraction these days."

The train—an antique steam locomotive called *Bethuselah*—wheezes back and forth along the old cliff-top line during the summer months, stopping at a few half-forgotten villages on the way. I expect the sun-seeking tourists who ride it in August think it's quaint. But *quaint* is one of those words that can tip easily into *eerie* once the weather turns and the dark of winter closes in. And yet, the train does still sometimes run in the off-season—cliff collapses and bonkers weather permitting. You'd have to be pretty bonkers yourself to use it then, though, which is why I'm huddling beside Violet, wrapped up against the icy wind in a coat and scarf, and muttering, "I've got a queasy feeling about this," as we wait for old *Bethuselah* to bring her mysterious visitor to town.

"And you really don't have any idea who it is?" Violet demands of the hotel manager, ignoring my queasiness and taking a crumpled bag of Mrs. Fossil's rum fudge from her pocket. "This special guest?"

"No, I do not," Mr. Mollusc snaps, turning to Violet to bristle his mustache directly at her. "And quite what business it is of *yours*, I don't know. I am here as an emissary of the Grand Nautilus Hotel, at the behest of Lady Kraken herself. Herbert Lemon is here to carry the bags and do as he's told. Remind me again, girl, why *you* are here."

Violet shrugs.

"Maybe I'm a trainspotter," she replies, with a sweet look of innocence that hardly suits her. "Here to spot a train."

"Pfft!" goes Mr. Mollusc. "Hardly! You're here to rubberneck at our VIP and stop the Lemon boy from doing his work, as usual. But I'm warning you, Violet Parma—Her Ladyship has commanded a Grand Nautilus welcome for this very special person, and you will *not* get in the way."

And he tries to look important as he wipes the remains of the "pfft!" off his mustache with a hanky.

"So, it really could be anyone?" says Violet, her eyes wondering. "Could be a film star! Or a sports champion, or"—she excitedly pops a piece of fudge in her mouth before offering the bag to me—"or a mysterious person with a dark past, whose arrival will spark a whole new adventure!"

The hotel manager frowns in annoyance as he slaps my hand away from the bag.

"No sweets on duty! And no dark pasts or adventures, thank you very much. If I had my way—Oh, what *is* that noise?"

The thumping sound, the one we noticed earlier, has been growing louder.

"It . . ." I start to say, with a definite uptick of the queasy feeling, "it sounds like footsteps. On the roof!"

"Nonsense!" Mr. Mollusc snorts, looking up at the creaky wooden canopy that covers the platform. "Why would anyone be up there? Above us? Walking toward that . . . that hole over there? Thumping and lumping along with the slow, uncertain, *awful* shuffle of a . . . of a . . ."

He gulps.

"Of a zombie?" I suggest, and the Mollusc stiffens with fright.

Slowly, the three of us look up at the windy gap in the platform roof as the . . . whatever-it-is . . . approaches.

Thump . . . thump . . .

Thump!

The sound comes to an abrupt halt right by the hole.

And nothing happens.

"Perhaps this *is* a ghost train, after all," Violet declares brightly, before chomping on another cube of fudge. "How exciting!"

"Oh, really!" Mr. Mollusc pulls himself together. "I'm sure there's a perfectly rational explanation for—"

And that's when, with a terrifying shriek of despair, the ghost appears!

CHAPTER 2

BETHUSELAH

O r rather, the ghost falls through the hole in the roof and lands on the platform with a thud. And we see that it's not a ghost at all, but . . .

"A seagull!" I cry, trying to sound like I knew that all along.

Sure enough, a scruffy white-and-gray seagull is flopping around in the leaves on the platform. It gives another piercing shriek and pecks ferociously at something blue wrapped tightly around its legs and one wing.

"Disgusting!" Mr. Mollusc cries, backing away. "Filthy thing!"

"It's not disgusting," Violet says. "It's *tangled*. Tangled up in an old plastic bag."

Without hesitation Violet pushes the bag of fudge into my hand and stoops down beside the stricken bird. I'm reminded, as it writhes around beside Violet, of just how enormous seagulls can be. Vi tries to grab the plastic but has to pull her hands back to avoid a vicious peck. Then, as the gull struggles once more—its one free wing thumping uselessly on the ground—Violet pounces, pinning the bird firmly but gently onto the platform. The seagull pecks at her furi- ously, but the sleeves of her too-big coat— borrowed once from my Lost-and-  Foundery and not yet returned—protect her.

"Don't just stand there, Herbie!" Violet gasps, struggling to hold the bird. "We've got to help it. Do you have something to cut the plastic off?"

"Cut it off?" Mr. Mollusc seems to be having as much trouble believing what he's seeing as if an actual ghost had appeared. *"Help* it? Don't be absurd, child! Seagulls are a nuisance. No more than vermin. Just kick it onto the railway line and let the train put it out of its misery. It'll be one fewer flying rat to deal with."

I rummage deep in my pockets as Violet glares daggers at the hotel manager. I wish I could use one of those daggers to free the bird. Instead, all I have to give Violet is the key to my toolbox.

"It's OK, it's OK," Vi whispers softly to the panicky gull as she saws at the twisted blue shopping bag with my key. "Ignore the horrible man. You'll soon be free."

I say nothing. I hate to agree with Mr. Mollusc, but seagulls *are* a nuisance and thieves, every one of them! And Eerie-on-Seagulls are the worst of all. I've lost more chips and doughnuts than I can remember to these pesky birds over the years. But, at the same time, I know Violet is right. We can't leave the poor thing to die a slow and plasticky death.

"Pah!" Mr. Mollusc says. "That's the problem with you goody-two-shoes types—you're always trying to be kind, even when it doesn't count. But that creature won't thank you, girl. When it's free, you're more likely to end up with a bleeding hand, to go with your bleeding heart."

The bag finally comes away, and the bird struggles harder now that its other wing is loose. Violet cries, "Stand back!" before lifting her hands to release the gull. It springs into the air, flapping furiously as it rushes across the platform and out into the sky.

"Being kind always counts," Violet says as she gets to her feet and faces the hotel manager. "One day it might be *you* who needs help from a stranger, and—"

But before Violet can finish, and without warning, the seagull reappears! It swoops straight at her, jabbing viciously with its beak, forcing her to cover her eyes with her hands. The bird hovers over her head, beating its wings and jabbing again and again as Violet cries in pain. Then, just as I'm finally getting my legs into gear so I can help, the great white bird flaps straight at *me*! With a final pterodactyl cry right in my face, it snatches the paper bag of fudge from my hand, beats its strong wings out into the sky above the station, and flies away toward the sea, a small scrap of blue plastic still caught around one leg.

"Violet!" I rush over to her. "Vi, are you OK?"

Violet lowers her hands. She has a nasty cut on her cheek and a look of shock on her face.

And that's when we hear a new sound—a horrible, wheezy rasping sound that, on investigation, turns out to be the noise Mr. Mollusc makes when he is laughing uncontrollably.

"Ah, *ack ack*!" he cackles. "Oh, dearie me . . . *ack*! This is just *too* good . . ."

He has to gulp in some air before he can continue.

"Maybe you've learned your lesson now, girl. You might think the universe dishes out rewards to do-gooders, but the seagull says otherwise. Ha! I hope you enjoy your dose of reality. Now, get yourself cleaned up—the train is arriving, and I don't want our special guest to arrive to a pool of blood. Eerie-on-Sea has a bad-enough reputation as it is."

All I can do is pass Violet a cleanish tissue—and give her a grin of encouragement—as a distant light grows in the tunnel and the echoing clamor of the approaching locomotive fills the air.

"Straighten your cap, Lemon!" Mr. Mollusc says to me, fiddling with his tie. "And try to look useful for once. Remember, there's no impression like a first impression."

"Even if the first impression is the worst impression," I mutter under my breath, but the Mollusc is too busy arranging his hair to notice.

"That looks nasty," I add to Vi, as she dabs her cheek.

She manages a small smile.

"I've had worse," she says. "And it was *still* the right thing to do."

"I know," I reply. "But it feels like a sign of bad things to come. Ever since I heard about this special guest, I've been having a . . ."

"A queasy feeling?" Violet finishes for me. "Yes, you said. But, Herbie, this could actually *be* the start of a new adventure. Aren't you at least a little bit excited?"

"Nope."

"Really? You aren't at all curious about who is on that train?"

"Nope," I say again.

"But . . ." Violet is clearly building up to a big argument to persuade me.

"I'm going to stop you right there, Vi," I say firmly, straightening my cap and giving my friend one of my most determined looks. "I'm doing NOPE-vember this year. I've been saying 'nope' to everything remotely adventurous all month, and I've still got two days to go. I'm here to carry bags and keep my head down, thanks. And after your nasty run-in with that seagull, I suggest you do the same."

"Herbie!" Violet cries, making her cheek bleed again.

"Nope!" I declare, passing her another tissue. "The sooner we get back to the warm fire in my Lost-and-Foundery, the better I will be, and that's that. Besides, here's the train."

With a rush of sooty smoke and a blast of steam whistle, *Bethuselah* eases into the station. The enormous train puffs to a standstill, wheezing like an old iron dragon with a chesty cough. I've never seen the locomotive up close before, and the black-and-red paintwork of its immense bulk looms over us. Great clouds of steam and smoke—as thick as any sea mist—engulf the platform, making Mr. Mollusc splutter into his handkerchief.

"Eerie-on-Sea!" calls a voice, and we dimly see the conductor, dressed in an old-fashioned uniform, step onto the platform and ring a handbell. "Eerie-on-Sea, and the end of the line!"

"Honestly!" gasps Mr. Mollusc, waving smoke from his face. "Only in this ridiculous town would I have to put up with such nonsense. A *steam* train, indeed! This infernal contraption belongs in a museum."

"Less of that, thank you." The conductor glares at the hotel manager, giving *Bethuselah*'s flank an affectionate pat. "Old Beth has years of life left in her yet, don't you, girl?"

The train emits a mighty *POOT* from her whistle, as if in reply.

"Now, all aboard if you're coming aboard," the conductor continues. "They're forecasting snow, and the last place you want to get stuck in is Eerie-on-Sea. All aboard!"

"We're not getting *on*," Mr. Mollusc snaps in reply. "We're getting someone *off*. A very important someone. Don't you have any passengers?"

The conductor looks back down the platform. No one emerges from the smoke and darkness.

"Funny, I thought there *was* someone," he says, with a shrug, "but I must be mistaken."

Then he signals to the train engineer, climbs back onboard, and slams the door behind him. With great deliberation, the mighty locomotive gasps out a vast puff of steam, and then another and another, as it begins to ease backward toward the tunnel.

"Stop!" Mr. Mollusc cries, starting after it. "What about my VIP?"

But the train gives a final, echoing whistle of farewell and is gone, leaving behind nothing but swirling clouds and an empty platform.

Except, wait—it's not entirely empty.

As the sea wind begins to clear the smoke, it seems that something might be there after all. A shape is becoming visible in the gloom—the shape of a solitary man, standing beside two suitcases.

"Oh!" Mr. Mollusc stops and straightens his tie again. "I *do* beg your pardon, sir. Are you expecting us? We are from the Grand Nautilus Hotel, sent to receive a special guest. Is it . . . is it you?"

"Well, well, well," comes a voice from the shape-of-a-man, "that's Godfrey Mollusc, unless I am very much mistaken. Ah, it is *so* good to be home."

Then the man steps forward into the uncertain light and raises his hat. I'm so shocked that I cry out an involuntary "NOPE!" before I can stop myself. Violet stiffens beside me, letting out a sharp gasp of her own.

Because, it seems, we *are* going to see a ghost today.

"Perhaps you remember me?" the man suggests, stepping farther into the light so that there can be no doubt at all. "I feel sure that you do. My name is Eels, Sebastian Eels."

CHAPTER 3

MENACE AND MISCHIEF

B ut are you sure?" says Wendy Fossil. "Sure it was *actually* him?"

"Yup!" I exclaim.

We're sitting in the main room of the Eerie Book Dispensary, beside the crackling fire, clutching mugs of fortifying hot chocolate while three pairs of eyes stare at us in disbelief.

"Of course we're sure!" says Violet, nearly spilling her cocoa over Erwin, the bookshop cat, who is trying without success to snooze on her lap. Jenny Hanniver, the owner of the Eerie Book Dispensary, is dabbing the wound on Violet's cheek with disinfectant.

"How could we not be?" Violet continues. "It was Eels all right, larger than life, just standing there on the platform, like nothing bad had ever happened, and like he wasn't to blame for it *all*!"

The three pairs of eyes turn to one another, clearly doubtful. The pair that belongs to Dr. Thalassi narrows at us beneath his bushy eyebrows. The doc is the town's medical man and the curator of the Eerie Museum, and I expect it's part of his job to narrow his eyes at things that don't sound likely. Then he switches his focus to Jenny, who is still dabbing Violet's wound.

"Would you like me to do that?" he asks. "I have my doctor's bag with me."

"But are you saying Eels *hurt* you?" Mrs. Fossil cries, before Jenny can reply. Mrs. Fossil, the town's only professional beach-comber, is the owner of the third pair of eyes—eyes that are as wide as empty buckets at the sight of the blood. "When he got off the train?"

"It wasn't Eels who did that," I explain. "Violet tried to make friends with a seagull, that's all."

"Most unwise," tuts the doc. "They can get very aggressive for food once the tourists have gone. In fact, the common herring gull is particularly noted for—"

"I don't care what the common herring gull is particularly

noted for!" Violet shouts, making Jenny sit back in alarm. "Didn't you hear what we said? Sebastian Eels has returned to Eerie-on-Sea!"

"But what did you *do*?" asks Mrs. Fossil.

"What *could* we do," I say, shrugging, "other than what we were told? I carried his fancy suitcases while Mr. Mollusc escorted him to the hotel as if he were royalty. He's there right now, I expect, in one of the finest rooms, pulling the wings off fairies or eating puppies with a cake fork, or whatever it is villains like him do for fun."

"He has a house in town," Dr. Thalassi says, narrowing his eyes again. "Why would he stay at the hotel?"

"Sebastian's house has been boarded up for most of last year," Jenny replies, finishing with Violet's cheek. "I doubt it's very comfortable right now. And wasn't there a break-in, recently? And a fire?"

I slurp my hot chocolate and catch Violet's eye. There was indeed a recent break-in at Sebastian Eels's house, which, er, might have been a *little* bit to do with us. And yes, perhaps things *did* get a teensy bit bonfirey. I slurp again, louder this time.

"Are these really the questions we should be asking?" says Violet then. "Where's he sleeping and is he comfy? This is Sebastian Eels we're talking about! What are we going to *do*?"

Dr. Thalassi gets to his feet. He strides over to the great marble fireplace and pokes the fire into an even cheerier glow. The light dances around us, reflecting off the countless spines of books that rise—shelf after shelf—to the midnight-blue ceiling, which is painted with stars. In the window, the mechanical mermonkey, whose job it is to choose books for you at the Book Dispensary of Eerie-on-Sea, sits hairy and awful on its pedestal, as if waiting for someone to answer Violet's question.

Instead, the three adults start talking among themselves, excluding us from the conversation. We hear phrases like "if he *is* back, then . . ." and ". . . definitely guilty of criminal behavior, so . . ." and even "perhaps we should go and find out what he has to say for himself." This last was from the doc and is met by nods of approval from the others.

"But wait!" Violet jumps to her feet, spilling Erwin onto the floor. Dr. Thalassi is already reaching for his coat. "You can't just go round there. Eels is *dangerous*! Shouldn't we call someone? Or . . . or something?"

"Who could we call?" the doc replies. "And what can we prove? Violet, we know the man has a questionable past, but let's not get carried away. He wouldn't return like this, in the open and on the train, if he were plotting some new mischief, now, would he?"

"But . . . !"

"No, Violet." The doc is firm. "Let's just keep an eye on him for the moment, and maybe have a quiet word if—and only if—he appears to be up to no good. Everyone deserves a second chance. Let's find out what he's doing here first, and then decide."

Violet flops back into the chair with a look of thunderous disbelief beneath her tangled dark hair.

"Oh, and, Herbie, about that clockwork-shell device of yours," the doc adds, pausing at the door as he pulls on his coat. "The one you left with me for repair? You should come and collect it. I fear it is damaged beyond even my expertise."

With this piece of distressing news, Dr. Thalassi leaves the shop, and now it's my turn to sag in my chair.

The shell the doc was talking about is none other than Clermit—my clockwork hermit crab and trusty mechanical sidekick. You might know about him already, if you've visited Eerie-on-Sea before and heard some of the stories about me. He's a wondrous little gadget who has helped me and Vi out of several tight spots. But he was smashed on our last adventure. Now it sounds like we may never be able to count on his help again.

"Come on, you two!" Jenny says, treating us both to a reassuring smile. "Don't look so glum. I know it's a shock, but the doctor is probably right about simply keeping an eye on Eels for now. In the meantime, I'll get you a Band-Aid, Violet, before you scowl so hard that scratch starts bleeding again."

"And I'll get the kettle back on," adds Mrs. Fossil, following Jenny out. "I could do with another cup of tea while I'm waiting for the tide to go out."

"Herbie, why don't they get it?" Vi demands as soon as the adults have left and we're alone. "After everything Eels has done, why are they so calm and breezy?"

And, suddenly, I think I understand.

"It's because they don't know what we know, Vi," I say. "I mean, not all of it. They get that he's done bad things, yes, but they didn't actually *see* everything we saw, did they?"

"What do you mean?"

"Well, think back to that time they rescued us from the wreck of the battleship *Leviathan*. They didn't get there till *after* Eels had said and done all the terrible things he said and did to get the malamander egg. They never saw any of the truly eerie stuff then, either. They know he's reckless and unpredictable, but I reckon they don't know how much of a villain he really is."

"But what about our Gargantis adventure?" Violet demands. "And all that happened with the Shadowghast lantern? Surely they saw enough then?"

I shrug.

"They weren't with us all the time. And sometimes they were hurt or distracted or enchanted by dark magic. It's us who have the adventures, Vi—you and me. Mrs. F, Jenny, and the doc, they just clean up after them and make the sandwiches. No, when it comes to Sebastian Eels, the others mostly only know what we tell them, and we never tell them *everything*, do we? At least, I don't."

"But Eels is a monster!" Violet cries. "The real monster behind everything awful that's happened to us. And behind the disappearance of my mum and dad. How can they *not* know?"

"Every adult was a child once," says a familiar feline voice, "but not every adult remembers."

Erwin, finally daring to jump back into Violet's lap, purrs his rumbliest purr.

"I'm not sure what that one means," I say, rumpling the cat's head with my knuckles. "But if you're saying grown-ups see the world differently, puss, then I'm with you."

"He fired a harpoon at me," Vi whispers, her face suddenly full of the many crimes of Sebastian Eels. "Remember? Tried to actually *kill* me, and only a book saved my life. And all Jenny can do is make hot chocolate and fetch a Band-Aid!"

I take another slurp, a good, long one.

"They are just doing what they think is best," I say. "I expect they don't want to worry us. But they'll keep an eye on Eels, Vi, that's for sure."

"It's not enough," Violet declares, thumping the arm of her chair and making Erwin bristle. "Sebastian Eels *is* up to no good, Herbie—he *has* to be. And it looks like it's up to us to find out what."

CHAPTER 4

MERIAM

You wish to do *what?*" Mr. Mollusc demands, looking down his nose at me.

It's a little while later, and I'm back at the Grand Nautilus Hotel, standing on the gleaming marble floor of the lobby. Violet is already in my Lost-and-Foundery, waiting while I ask the hotel manager an important question.

"I just wondered," I reply, tugging the front of my jacket flat and trying to look undeniable, "sir, if perhaps I could please possibly see Lady Kraken?"

I already know what his answer will be. No one sees Lady Kraken, unless—very, *very* occasionally—she summons them up to her rooms. But that summoning *has* happened to me before, and more than once, too. So, as I stand there in the royal porpoise blue and gleaming brass buttons of my Lost-and-Founder's uniform, trying to stare down the outrage on Mr. Mollusc's face, I hope against hope that I can somehow summon myself up to see her again now.

"It's, um," I add, playing my trump card, "it's for really important Lost-and-Founder business."

Mr. Mollusc leans down, lowering his face to mine until our noses almost touch.

"No," he hisses over me. "And if you don't get back behind your desk, boy, I'll report you lost myself and stuff you at the bottom of the odd shoe basket with the other useless things no one wants. Now go!"

And he points to the cubbyhole entrance of my Lost-and-Foundery. I slope off toward it, defeated, and let myself in.

"Told you it would be no good," I whisper to Violet, who was eavesdropping on all this from beneath my desk. "One does not simply walk into the Jules Verne Suite and demand an audience with Lady K."

"But we have to see her," Violet replies. "From what your Mr. Mollusc said at the railway station, it's clear Lady K knows why Sebastian Eels is here. She's the one who called him a VIP, isn't she? And sent us to meet him off the train?"

"First," I say, "he's not *my* Mr. Mollusc! And second, Lady

Kraken sent *me* to meet Eels off the train. You just came along to be nosy and save seagulls."

"Well, if we can't arrange a meeting with Lady Kraken," Violet continues, ignoring my correction, "we'll just have to go up there and ring her doorbell ourselves."

"What?"

"And since I already know you're about to have another of your queasy feelings, Herbert Lemon, I say we go up there right now. And don't you dare say 'nope'!"

I slump. I'd much rather stay down in my cellar, stoke up the stove, and spend the next day or two eating leftovers and talking it all over, but Violet is already checking to see if the coast is clear. Unfortunately for me, it is.

"OK." I sigh, opening my desk and letting her out into the lobby. "But Mollusc mustn't see you. Stay close!"

One person has already seen us, though, as we hurry across the lobby toward the gleaming hotel elevator. Amber Griss, the receptionist, gives us a tut of disapproval as she sees Violet with me. But it's a good tut, one I can work with, and I know she won't say anything. I give Amber a wink in return—one of my cheekiest—then I press the button to open the elevator door, and Vi and I step inside.

"Do you remember when you showed me the secret buttons?"

Violet says, tapping the dimpled control panel where six buttons—labeled G to 5—are displayed. "The ones that lead to all the hidden places the hotel guests aren't supposed to know about? There was one for Lady Kraken's private flat on the sixth floor. Let's use it now."

"Of course I remember," I reply. Then I add, with a shudder, "And I remember what happened next, too. So, today we'll just use the elevator like normal people who aren't doing something they shouldn't, Vi, and *walk* the rest of the way."

Ignoring Violet's obvious disappointment, I press the number 5 on the control panel, and the elevator doors slide shut.

"Sebastian Eels is actually here, Herbie," Violet says then, as we ascend. "In the hotel. Can you believe it?"

"I can believe it," I reply. "I'm just trying not to *think* about it, that's all. He's someone else we mustn't bump into."

With a *ping*, we arrive and step out onto the scallop-patterned carpet of the fifth floor. Ahead of us stretches a dark corridor lined with doors to guest rooms that are probably all empty at this time of year. I lead the way to a concealed flight of service stairs. We creep up them as quietly as we can to the sixth floor.

This part of the building is so strictly off-limits that even I have only been here a handful of times. Above us, crystal

chandeliers float like icebergs viewed from the bottom of the sea, and all along the stately corridor on the way to the Jules Verne Suite—Lady Kraken's private apartment—hang portraits of her seafaring ancestors, who look down on us with disapproval as we pass below.

"Are you sure about this?" I whisper to Violet when we reach the great wooden doors.

"Nope!" she declares with a mischievous look. Then she pulls the bell rope anyway.

From behind the doors comes the chime of a ship's bell.

After a moment, a small light bulb on a brass wall panel fizzes on, showing tiny curly letters saying:

COME IN

And the doors swing slowly open.

"So, you're back, are you?" comes a creaky voice from somewhere within the dust and darkness beyond. "You'd better have a thunderously good explanation for this, or there will be consequences. I'm surprised you dare show your face here at all."

"..." I say, wishing something more convincing would come

out of my mouth. Already I can sense my feet slipping into reverse and preparing to make a quick getaway.

"Well, don't keep me waiting!" snaps the voice again. "I am not known for my patience with visitors."

"Sorry to disturb you, Your Ladyship," says Violet, hesitatingly, "but Herbie said it would be OK."

There's a moment of silence from inside the room.

Then, with an electrical whir, the antique lady who lives here trundles forward in her bronze-and-wicker wheelchair, clicks on a small table lamp, and lets weak golden light wash over us like molasses.

"Herbert Lemon!" cries Lady Kraken. "And his girlfriend. What are *you* two doing here?"

"It's not . . ." I say, as I stumble into the room, propelled by Violet. "It's not *girlfriend*—one word—Your Ladyness," I explain. "It's more that she's a friend who is also a girl, so *two* words. And . . . and I didn't exactly say it would be *OK*. I think the word I used was *bonkers*, or it should have been, and anyway . . ."

"Stop wittering, boy!" Lady K waves me to silence with one spindly hand. With the other she flips a switch on the arm of her wheelchair, and the great doors of the Jules Verne Suite swing closed behind us. "Still a complete dunderbrain, I see. But now you're here, let me get a good look at you. And especially at Violet—your friend-who-is-a-girl."

"You know my name?" Violet says, blinking in surprise.

"Of course!" cries Lady Kraken. "It's my hotel, isn't it? I know everything that goes on. And if I don't, my Lost-and-Founder here is sworn to be my eyes and ears, and tell me all. Isn't that right, boy?"

"It is!" I squeak. "And, about that . . ."

"Now, Violet," Lady Kraken says, ignoring me and patting the seat of a nearby chair. "Come and sit beside me, and tell me all about yourself. Still climbing in through the cellar window, I hope?"

A wizened smile breaks out across her turtle face.

"You . . . y-you know about that, Your Ladyship?" Violet stutters.

"I do!" the lady replies. "And none of this high-and-mighty-ship nonsense, if you please. I just know that you and I are going to be great friends, my dear. You may call me Meriam."

And I can't help gawping at this. Lady Kraken has always treated me well, but also pretty roughly. Talking to her is a bit like being slapped about the face with a scented velvet glove, stuffed with twigs. But there's no poke in the ribs for Violet, no "dunderbrain" this, or "ninnyhammer" that. And I've *never* been invited to come and sit beside Lady K. Let alone call her by her first name. I didn't even know she had one!

"Would you care for some Turkish delight?" my ancient employer continues, pushing an open box of sugary cubes across the table to Violet. "I have it shipped in from Istanbul directly. One of the perks of living in a seaside town."

"Thank you," says Violet, looking at me in bewilderment as she takes a piece of candy. "M-Meriam. But the reason we've come is to say we're worried about someone who is staying in the hotel. And we thought you might be able to tell us about him."

"Sebastian Eels," I add, to make it clear. "You sent me to meet him off the train this morning."

"Oh, him!" Lady Kraken's eyes narrow, and her smile goes down at the edges. "The so-called author. Well, he was insistent about staying here, and he is a famous son of Eerie, despite being a bounder of the deepest stripe. But I don't mind rolling out a bit of red carpet for him if he's serious about what he's proposing for the town. And if he wants to turn over a new leaf and make amends, it won't be me who stops him."

"What is he proposing?" Violet asks quietly, the uneaten lump of Turkish delight becoming squashed between her fingers, "for the town?"

"Oh, well, you can ask him that yourselves," Her Ladyship

replies, skewering her own cube of the sweet jelly with one long fingernail and popping it in her mouth. "He's due any second. He can tell you all about it."

Then we hear a floorboard creak at the door of Lady Kraken's chambers, and the ship's bell chimes once more.

"Ah," says the hotel owner, "here he is now."

CHAPTER 5

TO SCARE
LITTLE CHILDREN

Violet looks at me in horror. I return the look. With interest!

We wanted information about Eels, not to be suddenly face-to-face with the man again, here, in a part of the hotel where we have no control.

"I think we should go," says Vi, standing abruptly. "Er, may we leave by the window?"

"No need!" declares Lady K, flipping the switch that opens the doors to her apartment. "You, dear Violet, are my guest. Mr. Eels will see me as I am, or not at all."

And now the doors are open.

The tall form of Sebastian Eels stalks into the room.

Even though he has a slight limp and is trying to look polite, our old enemy still radiates a distinct sense of malice—like a shark following a seal pup into the only entrance of a cave. Violet rushes to my side and grips my arm. And believe me, when the bravest person you know rushes to your side and grips your arm, it is NOT reassuring. Together we step back and wish the shadows could swallow us whole.

"Lady Kraken," says Eels, "thank you for seeing me . . . oh."

He stops as he notices us. His face goes rigid, and I finally get a good look at the man.

There are signs of our previous adventures all over him. His face, though still handsome, is haggard, and there is more shade beneath his eyes and lines on his brow than before. He flexes one of his hands painfully at his side, and I see the hint of burn marks there. Most disturbingly, there is an unhealthy tone to his skin, which even in this dim light has something indefinable of the deep sea about it.

Then, as we watch, Eels reaches around to scratch between his shoulder blades, at the place where . . . but no, I don't want to think about the terrifying *thing* that once sprouted there thanks to stolen magic. Eels sees me noticing, and a knowing smile wavers across his scarred lips.

"Herbert Lemon." Sebastian Eels nods in greeting, his voice a little cracked. "Violet Parma. Such a delight to see old friends again. Thank you for meeting me off the train this morning and carrying my bags. My health isn't what it once was."

And the smile dies a little as he adds:

"We really must have a proper catch-up sometime soon. So much unfinished business between us."

Beside me, Violet trembles. I can almost hear the storm of words that must be brewing in her brain—the words you need when you want to tell someone who has tried to kill you, who has tried to destroy everything you know and love, to GO. TO. BLAZES!

But Violet, for once, seems unable to speak.

"Sit, Mr. Eels," Lady Kraken commands, indicating a large armchair. "Welcome back to Eerie-on-Sea. You have been away a long time. At least"—and here she arches a brow—"so it seems. But there are many rumors about you and about what you've been up to. If even a fraction of it is true, I should ring for the police, not have you met off the train and allow you into my hotel. So, what have you to say for yourself?"

Sebastian Eels perches on the edge of the chair and folds his arms defensively. Then he turns toward Lady K, a little shamefaced.

"I confess, I have not been quite in my right mind this last year or so," he says, "and I may have caused a little trouble here or there—"

Violet reacts so violently to this, she almost pulls my arm out of its socket.

"But, I wonder," Eels continues, glancing back at us, "what people have been saying?"

"As for that"—Lady K bobs her turbaned head—"there is talk of plots and schemes, of stratagems and swindles, and even of criminality of a most exotic kind. I cannot, now I come to consider it, think of any *specifics*," Lady Kraken admits, "but the impression you have left in this town is one of downright dastardliness. So, have you been dastardly? And downrightly so?"

Sebastian Eels fiddles with his fingertips. As we watch, all the malice and evasiveness seem to drain out of him.

"I'm so sorry!" he cries suddenly, like a naughty schoolboy who has been caught throwing stones. "I . . . I have behaved in a most shameful way. I know it! And I . . . I've *hurt* people. But I promise, *I swear*, Lady Kraken, that I will never do it again."

"So, it's true?" Lady Kraken's face goes full bad-tempered turtle. "You confess to it all?"

Sebastian Eels seems to wilt further under the lady's glare, his eyes becoming watery. But then, regaining a little control, he takes a deep breath and nods.

"I am, as you know, a writer," he says, "and sometimes, we writers can get . . . carried away with our dreams, and be—shall we say—a little less considerate of others than we should. You may call that dastardly, if you wish, Lady Kraken, and I won't object. But I have learned my lesson!" Here he looks over to us again. "All my mad plans have been defeated, and I have nothing left now but the consequences of my actions, and a desire to set things right again."

And he ends this little speech with a feeble cough that suggests his insides are as sickly as his outsides.

"Indeed," Lady Kraken sniffs. "But how, pray, can we ever trust you again?"

Sebastian Eels sits up a little straighter.

"I had a good life here in Eerie-on-Sea," he says. "Once. Now I would like to make amends so that I may live that life again."

There is a silence at this. Then, with a crinkle, Lady Kraken relaxes in her chair and speaks again.

"Well, I daresay one is never too old to learn a lesson. And you do look dreadful, man! Have you seen the doctor?"

"Thalassi?" Eels says, alarmed. "Oh, I . . . I wouldn't like to bother him. I just need rest, that's all. I must be fit again, in time for the great reopening. And there is so much work to do! I meant what I said, Lady Kraken—I plan to win back the trust of the town, and no expense will be spared."

"Reopening?" I manage to squeak. "What is reopening?"

"Festergrimm's," Sebastian Eels says, as if that explains everything. "It has been closed for too long. I doubt there are many now who even remember it. But I believe it is a hidden treasure, which could—with the right kind of investment—be brought back to life, to the benefit of all. It might even be just the kind of attraction to draw visitors to Eerie-on-Sea in the winter months."

"And that would be good for the hotel," Lady Kraken adds, bobbing her head in approval, "and the town. It will be a fine thing to see Festergrimm's opened up again. Frightened the life out of me as a girl, it did. Such a strange and eerie place. Haunted, or so they say. Some even claim they saw the grotesques move, and not in the way intended."

"But what *is* Festergrimm's?" I ask. "I've never heard of it before."

"The waxworks gallery, of course!" Lady K cries. "Right in the heart of the town, though you wouldn't know it now. You have probably walked past it a hundred times, Mr. Lemon, and never even knew."

"The waxworks were famous once," Eels says, with a faraway look. "They tell the story of Eerie-on-Sea—every strange, twisty tale and blood-chilling legend is there, depicted in wax models. But, as I promised in my letter, I plan to add some new waxworks to the Festergrimm collection. And yours, Lady Kraken, will take pride of place. As will the waxy likenesses of anyone else I see fit to add."

He darts a venomous look our way at this, but Lady K doesn't seem to notice.

"A model of me!" she cries, clapping her hands together. "To scare the little children! Oh, I cannot wait to see it."

I turn to Violet, wondering if she has found her voice again, but she is still staring at Eels from beneath her wild hair, her mouth clamped shut.

"I think we should go now, Your Ladyness," I say. "Found-and-lostering to do. I mean, *lost-and-foundering*. So, er, bye!"

And I steer Violet toward the door and our escape.

"Oh, Herbie," Sebastian Eels calls, just as I'm clutching the doorknob.

I turn. Slowly. Lady Kraken seems to be lost in a chuckling conversation with herself, so she probably doesn't hear what Eels says next.

"Talking of lost things needing to be found, Herbert Lemon, don't forget you have some property of mine to return."

"I . . . I do?"

"Oh, yes." Eels smiles, but only with his mouth. "I will come to your Lost-and-Foundery to collect it very soon. I just know you will have kept it safe."

I try a smile of my own, but a gulp gets there first. I don't know what the man is talking about!

"And if you haven't, boy," Eels adds, lowering his voice and letting full, undisguised hatred blaze from his eyes, "the wax-works gallery will be getting a new exhibit sooner than anyone thinks."

Then he turns back to Lady K and does his feeble cough again.

I slip out of the door faster than you can say *Madame Tussauds*, pulling Violet along behind me.

CHAPTER 6

BAGFOOT

....

I t's only when we're out of the hotel and standing on the
rainy cobblestones of the promenade that Violet finds her
voice again.

"Lady Kraken is just like the others!" she says. "She knows
Eels is bad, but she doesn't know *how* bad. And he's already won
her over, with this whatever-it-is he's planning to reopen."

"I've never even heard of Festergrimm's," I reply. "A waxworks gallery, here in Eerie-on-Sea! I wonder where it is?"

"Herbie! That doesn't matter. The point is, what are we going
to *do*?"

"Well, I know what I'm going to do," I reply. "I'm going to
avoid my Lost-and-Foundery for a bit. If Eels really is going to

ring my bell today, he can talk to the CLOSED sign. I don't have *anything* of his."

There's a flapping sound and a *whoosh* as a large, tatty seagull swoops overhead. A white dropping the size of a fried egg spatters across the cobblestones at Violet's feet as the bird swings around to land on the seawall. He tips his head to one side and looks at us with a beady yellow eye.

"It's that same seagull!" Violet cries. Sure enough, a scrap of blue plastic bag is still tangled around the gull's leg, flapping in the wind. "Shoo! Buzz off, you . . . you . . . *bagfoot!*"

But instead of buzzing off or shooing, the gull screeches at Violet, and a second Eerie-on-Seagull swoops in and lands beside him. Now they are both tipping their heads at us.

"Looks like Bagfoot's found a friend," I say. "He's probably been telling the other seagulls about your fudge."

"Well, he can stop," Violet says, glaring at the seagulls. "Thanks to him I don't have any fudge at all now."

"We shouldn't hang around here, then," I say. "The longer we do, the more it'll look to a hungry seagull like we're having a picnic. Let's go somewhere Bagfoot can't and work out what to do next."

"The book dispensary," says Vi, leading the way. "I want to tell Jenny what we just heard. Maybe she can tell us about this Festergrimm place."

But when we arrive at the Eerie Book Dispensary, Jenny is nowhere to be seen. There is, however, a strong whiff of burning fur and hot electronics in the air, which suggests a customer has recently consulted the mermonkey. Jenny is probably upstairs somewhere, helping them find their book. Violet flops onto one of the big armchairs and stares into the blazing fire, fiddling nervously with the strip of brown Band-Aid on her cheek.

I flop down opposite her and take off my cap. It feels like it's time for one of my reassuring comments.

"Maybe it's not as bad as you think, Vi," I say. "Sebastian Eels being back in town, I mean. Maybe, in the end, it will all be OK."

"Really?" Violet looks unconvinced. "How do you work that out?"

"I just mean," I explain, "that it's not like everyone thinks Eels is *good* all of a sudden. And arriving like this, in the open, at least means he's not in disguise again. If he really wants to reopen some moldy old waxworks museum as a favor to Lady K and to help out the town, then maybe we should just let him. And if he *does* get up to mischief again, well, everyone will be on to him in a moment. He won't last five minutes."

"'Mischief'?" Violet snorts. "Herbie, this is Sebastian Eels we're talking about. This waxworks business will be cover for some dark doings that go way beyond 'mischief'—you can bet on it."

Erwin jumps onto Violet's lap. He looks at her as if unsure whether he'll be stroked or bounced onto the floor like last time. Violet strokes him, but instead of the usual purr, Erwin flattens his ears suddenly and hisses at the shop door. With a *DING* of the shop's bell, a customer walks in.

"Welcome to the Eerie Book Dispensary," says Violet automatically, getting to her feet and putting Erwin down. "Have you come to consult the marvelous, mechanical mermonk . . . ?"

Her voice trails off.

"So, Violet Parma, you can still speak," says Sebastian Eels, removing his hat as he enters the shop and revealing his unwelcome identity. "I was beginning to think all our adventures together had left *you* damaged, too."

And he reaches around to scratch between his shoulder blades again.

"What do you want here?" Violet demands, her voice little more than a harsh whisper.

"Want *here?*" says Eels. "I don't want to be *here* at all. I just want Herbert Lemon to return what's mine. Are you planning to be in your Lost-and-Foundery today, boy? Or should I tell the hotel manager you are putting your feet up by the fire and waiting for Jenny to bring cake, despite there being lost property to return?"

I jump up and jam my cap back on.

"Nope!" I say. "I mean, no—no need to tell anyone." Then I add, in a voice that sounds braver than I feel, "But I'm sure I don't have anything that belongs to you. I think I'd remember!"

"Oh, you remember all right." Eels steps forward, looming over us. Any trace of the weakness we saw in him earlier is gone. "And I want it back! I swear I will not be stopped by you meddling kids again."

"You shot me!" Violet yells then, unable to contain her outrage any longer. "With a harpoon! Why should we ever believe *anything* you say?"

"What's this about a harpoon?" comes a voice, and Jenny returns from upstairs. She stops in her tracks when she sees who we're talking to. Behind her are Dr. Thalassi and Mrs. Fossil. All three of them stare openmouthed at Sebastian Eels. Each of them, I notice, is holding a book in their hands.

"It's nothing," says Eels, forcing a smile. "We were just reminiscing about old times, weren't we, Violet?"

"Do you have to stand quite so close," Dr. Thalassi says, "when you are reminiscing?"

And the doc, who does a good looming himself when he

needs to, strides into the room and comes to a halt between Sebastian Eels and the front door. Jenny walks over to us and puts a hand on each of our shoulders. Even Mrs. Fossil, who wouldn't say *boo* to a goose unless the goose asked her to, enters the room, thrusts her hands into the pockets of her waxed coat, and rocks back and forth on her boots, glaring at the disgraced author with the ferocious eye of a beachcomber spotting plastic in a rock pool.

Sebastian Eels is surrounded.

Suddenly, all the threat leaks out of him. He shrinks, becoming crooked and ill-looking again.

"Listen," he says, with a sickly grin. "I . . . I'm not here to cause trouble."

"Not cause trouble?" Dr. Thalassi bellows. "You *are* trouble! I wonder how you even dare show your face in Eerie-on-Sea again."

Eels backs away into a corner, tripping over a pile of books and spilling them everywhere.

"And I'm still waiting to hear about this harpoon," Jenny declares. "If you hurt Violet, so help me, I'll . . . I'll . . ."

"So will I!" Mrs. Fossil blurts out, with a squeak of her wellies. "With knobs on!"

Eels shrinks farther into his corner.

"No, I . . . I . . . *promise*," he pleads. "I promise I'm not here to hurt anyone. Look, I know I have done some bad things, and let myself get carried away with mad schemes, but I'm truly sorry! We were friends once, we four. Is there no way we can be friends again?"

The three adults look at one another.

"Jenny," Eels says, "surely you haven't forgotten all those times we spent together? Here in the bookshop? I was one of your best customers. I even helped you fix the mermonkey once. How is the creaky old thing, by the way? Still smoking from the left ear, is he?"

"Oh, Sebastian . . ." Jenny closes her eyes at the memories but clenches her fists.

"And Wendy!" Eels says quickly, opening his arms wide toward Mrs. Fossil, "have you forgotten the hours we spent together, beachcombing and finding all sorts of things? And I saved you from the quicksand that time. Remember?"

Mrs. Fossil blinks at him.

"Well . . ." she says, "well, yes, I suppose you did help me once. But we weren't exactly *friends* . . ."

"And the great Dr. Thalassi!" Eels turns now to the doc. "Still polishing your old bones, I imagine. Up at the museum? I do so miss our friendly discussions . . ."

"Stop this, Sebastian!" Dr. Thalassi commands, earning himself a flash of annoyance from Eels. "You can't just pretend

things are the way they used to be. Trust lost is the hardest trust to gain, and if you want to regain ours, you can start by keeping away from Violet and Herbie."

Eels looks at each of us in turn. Then, amazingly, he sinks down onto his knees among the spilled books and clasps his hands together.

"I promise!" he says. "I *swear* that I am a changed man. Just give me the chance to prove it."

Dr. Thalassi steps toward him.

So does Jenny Hanniver.

Mrs. Fossil approaches, too, followed by Violet and then me.

Soon the five of us are looking down at the villain of Eerie-on-Sea. It's not often that I, Herbert Lemon—Lost-and-Founder at the Grand Nautilus Hotel—get the chance to do a spot of looming of my own, but even I manage to throw some shade over the wretched Sebastian Eels.

"What do you think?" Dr. Thalassi asks the rest of us.

"I think I wouldn't trust this scoundrel with a paper clip," Jenny replies.

Mrs. Fossil shrugs. "But he does look terrible."

Eels coughs, pathetically.

"I'm not sure we can actually *force* him to leave town anyway," says the doc regretfully, though the look on his face suggests he'd like to try.

"But I don't want him here!" Violet declares. "He's a danger to everyone."

Erwin hisses, his ears as flat as a bookshelf.

And I go *Boo!* but only inside my head.

Then Jenny Hanniver says, "I have an idea."

CHAPTER 7

TRIAL BY MERMONKEY

S ebastian," says Jenny, "do you know what we were doing just now? Dr. Thalassi, Wendy, and I were consulting the mermonkey, to see what book it would choose for each of us. We were hoping for inspiration to help deal with your unwelcome return."

"Oh?" says Eels, a pathetic little ray of hope in his face.

"You may think the mermonkey is just a quaint Eerie tradition," Jenny continues, "but I've followed its peculiar recommendations for years, and its books have changed me—made me a better person, page after page, title after title. Maybe that's why I'm standing here, surrounded by friends and with ten thousand books behind me, while you grovel in the dust."

Eels blinks expectantly.

"I trust the mermonkey picked something nice for you all," he says. "Something good and . . . and forgiving."

"It did not." Dr. Thalassi gathers his bushy eyebrows like a thundercloud, as he raises the book in his hand for us all to see. "*Tales of Ghoulish Horror*," he says, intoning the title like a voice from the grave, "by Edgar Allan Poe."

Sebastian Eels gives a yelp and clutches at his collar.

"As for me," says Jenny, patting a book-shaped bulge in her pocket. "I'd rather not reveal what was chosen. But let's just say it does not leave me feeling warm and fuzzy about you, Sebastian, or in the mood to forgive and forget."

"Well, I got a nice Agatha Christie!" Mrs. Fossil declares, waving her book for all to see. "A Miss Marple mystery, too. And that can only mean one thing."

"Please!" Eels looks desperate. "Please give me a chance to prove myself!"

Jenny stares hard at him. Then she glances at the doc, who shrugs as if to say, *It's up to you.*

"Sebastian Eels," says Jenny then, "we may never trust you again. But as for giving you a second chance, we will leave that to the mermonkey. Will you submit to it? Will you let it choose a book for you, knowing that its choice may seal your fate?"

Sebastian Eels looks terrified now. But he nods his head.

The front door of the Eerie Book Dispensary is locked and the CLOSED sign put up. We are all of us—that is Dr. Thalassi, Jenny Hanniver, Mrs. Fossil, Violet, and me—standing in a ring around Sebastian Eels, as he faces the mermonkey.

The mermonkey leers back at him, hairy and strange, as it holds out its battered top hat for a coin.

"Is this really necessary?" Eels says, trembling slightly. He looks greener and sicklier than ever. "Perhaps I could just make a donation . . ."

"This is your one chance," booms the doc. "Stop sniveling and pay up. How much we leave you alone to rebuild your sorry life here in Eerie will depend on what happens next. Now get on with it."

Sebastian Eels rummages in his coat pockets, looking at each of us in turn. If he's after sympathy, he'll be disappointed. He pulls out a handful of coins and—after a hesitation—drops one in the hat with a *plop.*

Nothing happens.

He drops in another and then another.

With each coin, the hat creaks a little lower on the mechanical creature's arm, but still nothing happens.

"Oh, well." Eels tries a chuckle. "Seems to be on the blink again. I'll go home and give you a chance to fix it . . ."

Dr. Thalassi grabs Eels's wrist—the one attached to the hand full of coins—and squeezes it over the hat. Eels gives a squeak, and his hand springs open to let a shower of coins tumble in. The hat sinks farther until . . .

There's a click.

The arm begins to rise again, jerkily as the gears engage, clicking up and up till the hat is tipped over the monkey's head. The coins rattle down inside the mechanism, and the mermonkey's eyes light up. The creature—as if seeing who is there—jerks back.

Then it starts to scream.

The air fills again with the stink of old electronics and hot workings. As Eels stands before it, head bent, the mermonkey clicks and clacks with one crooked finger on its battered old typewriter—typing out the code that will indicate the chosen book. Then, as suddenly as it began, the creature retracts its typing hand, extends the hat once more to the "try me" position, and its eyes wink out.

There's a *TING*, and the prescription card flies out from the typewriter and hits Eels in the face.

"Ow!"

Violet picks it up and holds out the code for us all to see:

2 - 1 - N - Cr - 66

"I'll go and get it," says Violet, with delight.

"No!" Eels snarls, with a sudden return of his old forcefulness. He snatches the card from her. "If we have to go through this ridiculous charade, at least allow me to walk myself to the gallows."

"Very well," replies Dr. Thalassi. We step back and follow Eels as he sets off in a foul temper farther into the shop.

If you've been to Eerie-on-Sea before, you might remember how to read the mermonkey's code. The first number is the floor the book is on, so we escort Eels upstairs to floor 2. The second number gives the room on that floor, and 1 indicates the room at the front, overlooking Dolphin Square. When we get there, Eels is so angry that he grabs the bamboo steps and fixes them to the rail on the north wall—*N* in the code—with a *BANG* of fury. He'll need those to climb to the shelf painted crimson, which is what the *Cr* means. It's only as he climbs that he starts to tremble again, and his anger melts away..

"It's not fair!" he complains. "The mermonkey is just a machine. Why should I be judged by its random typing?"

"If it's just a machine," Jenny Hanniver replies, "why are you shaking so much? Now, count!"

The last part of the code is the number 66. Eels will have to reach this number by counting the books on the crimson shelf from left to right. We watch him as he counts, checking there's no cheating.

". . . sixty-three, sixty-four, sixty-five . . ." he says aloud.
"Sixty-six," he finishes, his finger resting on the spine of a book.
He freezes as he sees it, though it's too far for us to read the title.

"Well?" demands the doc. "Bring it down."

Sebastian Eels throws us a look of hatred. Then he starts
tugging the book, using both hands.

"It's stuck," he says. "Too many books wedged in. So sloppy,
Jenny, to treat books . . . like . . . *this*!"

With a final tug, the book comes free and flies out of Eels's
hands. It hits the shelves on the wall opposite and falls open on
the floor, its pages bent.

Violet darts over and snatches it up, keen to see the guilt of
Sebastian Eels written all over the cover.

But now it's her turn to freeze.

"No!"

"Oh, yes," says Sebastian Eels, sliding down the ladder and
turning to us in triumph.

"What is it!" I cry. "What's the book?"

Violet holds it up for us all to see.

CHAPTER 8

HUMBUG

A *Christmas Carol*," says Wendy, reading the title aloud, "by Charles Dickens."

"Give me that," the doc replies, taking the book and checking under the dustcover to see if some other title is concealed beneath. It isn't.

"Interesting choice," says Eels, with a new spring in his step. He plucks the book from Dr. Thalassi's hand and starts flicking through it. "I'm Scrooge, I suppose, learning the error of my ways thanks to three ghosts. Heh! That'll be you three, then: the Ghosts of Christmas Past, Present, and—if the face of old Thalassi is anything to go by—a miserable Christmas

Yet To Come. Heh, heh, I'll take that. Mad-haired Violet can be Fezziwig, and Herbie Lemon is Tiny Tim! Ha! It's *perfect*."

"This doesn't mean we suddenly trust you . . ." Jenny begins, clearly struggling to find a different meaning for the mermonkey's choice, but Eels interrupts.

"Oh, forget it, Jenny," he snaps. "Your little game is over. What else can this particular book mean? I said I was here to turn over a new leaf, and the mermonkey agrees. So, bah humbug to the lot of you!"

With this, he slips the copy of *A Christmas Carol* into his pocket and strides out of the room with a final "Humbug!" over his shoulder. By the time we get down to the main shop, Sebastian Eels has gone, leaving a bad feeling in the air and the front door swinging shut.

"Is that it?" Violet demands. "*That's* how we're deciding to treat Sebastian Eels? And he can just walk out of here now, and it's all OK?"

"It's not OK," Mrs. Fossil says. "But the mermonkey . . ."

"Oh, to blazes with the mermonkey!" snaps Dr. Thalassi, making Jenny Hanniver look at him sharply. "It *is* just a machine. This doesn't change anything."

But he looks as unsure as anyone else about what to do next.

"The mermonkey is the heart of my shop," Jenny insists,

"and I trust its choices. *A Christmas Carol* is probably the most famous book about second chances there is, so perhaps . . . perhaps Sebastian *can* redeem himself, after all."

"Hmmph," Dr. Thalassi grunts, snatching up his coat in disgust and wrapping his scarf around his neck. "We'll see about that."

Violet flops down in front of the fire again, looking more dejected than ever.

"Of all the books," she says, "how could such a villain be prescribed *that* one?"

Prrp!

Erwin is sitting beside the fireplace, playing with a crumpled-up ball of paper. He picks up the ball in his teeth, jumps onto Violet's lap, and drops it in her hands.

"Hot!" Violet cries, as she takes the smoldering paper and pats out the glowing edges. She unravels it. "Oh, thanks, puss," she says, when she sees what it is. "Eels's prescription card from the mermonkey, thrown on the fire on his way out. *Not* a souvenir I want to keep."

She crumples it up once more and tosses it into the log basket. Erwin pounces and gets it out again.

"Whichever way you look at it," says Mrs. Fossil, ignoring the cat's antics, "that rotter has been tested by the mermonkey. And passed!"

"What's Festergrimm's?" I ask then, thinking that a change of subject might be welcome about now. "Does anyone know?"

"Oh!" Mrs. Fossil goes as white as sea-foam.

"Now that's a name I haven't heard for many years." Jenny blinks in surprise. "It dates back to before I came to the town. Fancy you knowing about that, Herbie."

"But I *don't* know about it," I say. "That's the point."

And so, I tell the others what Sebastian Eels said to Lady Kraken about his plan to reopen the waxworks gallery as a gift for the town.

"Oh!" says Mrs. Fossil again, sinking into the armchair beside Violet.

"Are you OK, Mrs. F?" Violet asks, but the beachcomber seems unable to say anything right now.

"Festergrimm is not a name likely to inspire joy," says Dr. Thalassi. "Not in Eerie-on-Sea. But Festergrimm's Eerie Waxworks was indeed a tourist attraction at one time, though it was boarded up and forgotten long ago. I'm told the waxwork models were bad, but all the more terrifying for that. They say the place was finally shut down because a tourist died of fright in there."

Mrs. Fossil jumps in her seat.

"Wendy, what is it?" says Jenny gently. "Do you remember the waxworks gallery? You're Eerie born and bred—maybe it's somewhere you went to, when you were a girl?"

"*Went* there?" Mrs. Fossil looks at Jenny Hanniver with disbelieving eyes. "Well, yes, but . . ."

"Then you must know where it is," says Violet excitedly. "Festergrimm's? You could show us?"

"Of course I know where it is," the beachcomber replies. "I only wish I didn't! It's right opposite my Flotsamporium. I'm supposed to keep an eye on it."

"Really?" I ask. "Why?"

"Because I'm . . . I'm the caretaker," Mrs. F admits. "I have the key to Festergrimm's Eerie Waxworks."

⚙

Shortly afterward, we're standing outside Mrs. Fossil's beachcombing shop, looking at the boarded-up building in the center of the square known, ironically, as Fargazi Round. The doc and Mrs. F are with us, but Jenny has stayed behind to mind her bookshop.

"I always thought this was just an abandoned house," I say,

looking at the old timber building with new interest. It is completely sealed, and judging by the age of the peeling posters glued up on the shutters, it has been for decades. "It's hard to imagine tourists coming here, queuing up outside, and paying to go in."

"This building is older than you might think," Dr. Thalassi explains. "It was some kind of toy shop once, long before the waxworks gallery was set up. It'll be empty now, of course. I wonder where the old waxwork effigies went. I would have gladly taken some for the museum."

"So, do you have that key?" Violet asks Mrs. Fossil, rattling the handle of the locked door.

"You . . . you really want to go in?" Mrs. Fossil asks. "Just thinking about this place gives me the heebie-jeebies! Wouldn't you rather come to my place for tea and a bit of cake . . . ?"

"You don't have to come with us, Mrs. F," says Violet, putting her hand on the beachcomber's arm. "Not if it bothers you."

"No, it's all right, my dear." Mrs. F pats Violet's hand. "It wouldn't be right to let you go in there alone. It's just . . ."

"Yes?" says Violet.

But Mrs. Fossil shakes her head. Then she reaches above a wooden beam on her own shop front and pulls out a large brass key that was concealed there, covered in damp leaves and cobwebs.

"Don't look at me like that, Doc!" The beachcomber blushes

as Dr. Thalassi frowns at this not-very-secure hidey-hole. "I may be the caretaker of this awful place, but that doesn't mean I have to keep the key in my own home. I just wonder what you're hoping to find, Violet," she adds, wiping the key clean on her sleeve. "After all this time."

"I'm hoping to find whatever it is Sebastian Eels is hoping to find," Violet replies, taking the key. "I don't believe for a moment he's just looking for a harmless business opportunity. Do you?"

And she unlocks the old wooden doors to the waxworks museum without waiting for an answer.

CHAPTER 9

FESTERGRIMM'S
EERIE WAXWORKS

W e have to push against a snowdrift of mail that has piled up behind the doors to get them open. Weak November light streams into the building, conjuring shadows and strange objects that our minds struggle to understand. Then I gasp as I see a horrible leering face looking out at me.

"Heebie-jeebies!" Mrs. Fossil cries, catching sight of it at the same time.

"That'll be one of the waxworks, I imagine," says Dr. Thalassi, calmly stepping inside. "Fascinating! So, there are still some left, after all."

We follow him inside, Mrs. F entering last.

The gallery is one large open space. There is a counter with an antique cash register just inside the doors. Behind it are dingy shelves filled with dusty trinkets and abandoned souvenirs. More human figures become visible in the gloom—some shrouded in dust sheets, while others stare at us with dead glass eyes in hideously distorted faces.

"Creepy!" Violet says, approaching one waxwork figure, who seems to have pride of place. He has a long, lank beard over a tattered monk's habit and is holding a tall staff with a fish-shaped bottle hanging off the end. On the old man's face is an expression of fury, and emerging from his knobbly, misshapen head is a broken light bulb covered in cobwebs. "Hey, I think I recognize this one."

"That's old Saint Dismal," the doc says, chuckling. "Patron Saint of Calamitous Weather and First Fisherman of Eerie-on-Sea."

Dr. Thalassi pulls the dust sheet off another figure, revealing a pirate captain in a swashbuckling outfit, with pistols and a cutlass in her hands. She wears a long coat of a plummy color, to match the feather in her wide-brimmed hat.

"Purple Pimm!" the doc declares, clearly enjoying himself. "After her father was executed by the king, she turned rogue, and as captain of the *Hy Brasil* became Eerie-on-Sea's most infamous buccaneer."

"Wow!" I say. "Is that sword real? And was she really so ugly?"

"It's a real sword, all right," replies the doc, "but as for the ugliness, my guess is this model of Hester Pimm was once left out in the sun so long, she started to melt. Look, one eye is definitely lower than the other."

"So horrible," says Mrs. Fossil, with a wobble in her voice.

"What are the Eerie waxworks made of?" I ask, prodding the greenish, flubbery hand of Captain Pimm. "Ear-y wax?"

Violet pulls off another shroud to reveal a tall, overfed figure with wispy side whiskers and a gold chain. The man has an expression of disdain, spoiled by the fact that his nose has dropped off. A sign at his feet reads:

STANDING BIGLEY, ERSTWHILE MAYOR OF EERIE-ON-SEA

"I was expecting something a bit different," Violet admits. "I thought waxworks were usually Queen Victoria and Elvis Presley. You know, famous people."

"Not at Festergrimm's," Dr. Thalassi replies. "This place was designed to tell the strange tales of our town. No need for kings and queens when you have the legends of Eerie-on-Sea."

"What's this?" I ask, pushing farther into the gloom, to where a large wooden panel is leaning against the wall. I pull out the pocket flashlight I always carry and flick it on. A sculpted yellow face looks back at me, its eyes like lamps. On one side of the face is the word FESTERGRIMM'S in faded carnival colors, while EERIE WAXWORKS is on the other. There are light bulbs poking through the letters at regular intervals, but most of them seem to be broken.

"That's the old sign." Mrs. Fossil approaches cautiously. "It was above the front door once. I had it taken down years ago, before it could blow down."

"There's something behind it," Vi says, peering around. "It looks like a . . . a bumper car? No, more of a small train carriage. Like on a roller coaster."

With an effort, the doc shifts the sign out of the way, revealing what does indeed appear to be three small open carriages fixed to a track. The track extends forward and then descends quickly, vanishing into a hole in the floor behind a tattered black curtain.

"Most of the waxworks gallery is underground," Mrs. Fossil explains. "You have to ride on that little train to see it."

"Fascinating!" says Dr. Thalassi.

"Now that really *is* like a ghost train," says Violet.

At the word *ghost*, Mrs. Fossil gasps, steps back, and grabs someone's arm for reassurance. When she realizes it's the arm of the waxwork Saint Dismal, she releases it with another cry.

"Well!" the doc declares, looking around and appraising everything we have found with the experienced eye of a man who is at home with old and collectible objects. "I don't know what any of this says about Sebastian Eels, but I'm amazed to see so much still here. I hate to admit it, but there's huge potential in this place. Someone could indeed make a great tourist attraction with all this. It's just a shame it has to be Sebastian."

He turns to Mrs. Fossil. "And there's more below, you say?"

"Plenty more," Mrs. Fossil admits from the safety of the door. "Though if you want to see that, you'll have to do it without me. I'm going back to my warm kitchen now. If you wouldn't mind replacing the key when you've finished, Doctor, I'll be off."

And she hurries across the square back to her shop.

"She's really frightened of this place," Violet says, watching her go.

"Indeed," Dr. Thalassi agrees. "She seems an odd choice of caretaker."

I find my eyes drawn to the black curtain where the little train track disappears underground. It seems a shame to leave without taking at least a peek down below. There might be more pirates! Or something I've never seen before and may never see again.

I take a step onto the track and carefully lower myself down a few railroad ties, descending into the gloom. I get a twinge of queasiness in my stomach, but I ignore it. The waxworks are pretty creepy, it's true, but after some of the things I've seen on my adventures with Violet, I'm not going to let a few knobbly models and glass eyes bother me. I pick my way down farther, until I am standing in front of the black curtain.

Which moves. Ever so slightly.

There's a definite draft coming from below—moving air that

smells of decay and the passage of too many years of neglect. My hand pauses as I reach for the curtain, and the queasiness doubles.

"Just a peek," I say to myself. "Come on! Violet will be impressed."

I part the curtain and peer behind it, thrusting the beam of my flashlight into the dark beyond.

There are more waxworks here, in alcoves in the walls of a tunnel that the train would once have traveled down. A few of the models have sagged and collapsed, but there is one that catches my eye. It looks like a fisherman with wild scraggly whiskers, clutching a net. He's positioned so that he would look down on to the passengers of the train as they pass below, holding the net as if to catch them. He must surely have been a terrible sight once. Now, though, he's just one of the many tumbledown exhibits Eels will have to fix up if he's going to get this place working again.

I switch off my flashlight and let go of the curtain.

And hear a sound.

A creaking, metallic sound.

Before I know what I'm doing, I open the curtain again and turn the flashlight back on. I see the scraggly bearded fisherman again. And, before my disbelieving eyes, he turns his head to look at me.

CHAPTER 10

ROBOT

....

"Poor Herbie," soothes Mrs. Fossil as she clatters the kettle onto the hot plate and turns up the heat. "I knew no good would come of going to that terrible place."

We're in the Flotsamporium, among the baskets of beach-combed bits, jumbled clutter-boxes, and heaped-up, tide-rolled knickknackery that are Mrs. Fossil's treasures and her trade. The air is heavy with the smell of dried-up seawater, salty woodsmoke, and the sweet promising tang of new-made fudge.

"But what made you shout like that?" Violet asks me. "And why were you going into that tunnel on your own?"

"I wasn't *going* in," I reply, straightening my cap. "I was *looking* in. There is a difference, you know. And you would have shouted, too, if you'd seen one of the wax people move!"

"Oh, was that it?" says Dr. Thalassi with a chuckle, as he enters the shop behind us after locking up the waxworks gallery. "Never mind, Herbie—it's easy to let your imagination go in a place like that."

And he slaps me on the back, sending my cap tipping forward over my eyes.

"It wasn't my imagination . . ." I begin, but Violet nudges me in the ribs.

I look at her, and her eyes say, *Let's talk about this later*, so I clam up.

Mrs. Fossil—no longer in her coat, but wearing an apron patterned with starfish—is slicing a tray of fudge into blocks of sweet delight. The cold light of November's end is turned to rainbow by the hundred jars of sea glass in the shop window. The warmth of the Flotsamporium envelopes me as the kettle starts to sing.

"Vanilla or rum?" asks Mrs. F, bringing two bowls of fudge toward us. And my fright finally melts away. I must have been mistaken about what I saw in the tunnel as I waved my flashlight around.

Mustn't I?

"I wonder which flavor seagulls like best?" Violet says, with a wry look.

"Seagulls?" Mrs. Fossil looks confused, but Violet doesn't explain.

"Do you have anything about Festergrimm's at the museum?" I ask the doc. "About its history? For example, how it ended up with such a funny name?"

"Festergrimm?" Dr. Thalassi replies. "Yes, it is a bit strange, I suppose. But that was someone's actual name once upon a time, long before the waxworks gallery. Have you not heard the legend of Festergrimm before? I suppose not many have these days. It was a big deal in Eerie once, and, yes, I do have more information about it in the museum."

"Another legend of Eerie-on-Sea," Violet says, glancing at me again.

"So," I say, as I bite into a cube of melty vanilla fudge, "what *is* the legend exactly?"

"Ah!" The doc smiles, settling down and accepting a steaming teacup on a saucer from Mrs. Fossil. "Now, I won't pretend to have all the facts at my fingertips, Herbie, but hundreds of years ago a man named Ludovic Festergrimm came to live in Eerie-on-Sea. He was an inventor and clockwork-toy maker who once had a workshop in that very building we just visited. He was famous for his mechanical devices until, one day, tragedy struck: the clockwork maker's only daughter went missing. She was never found, and the grief drove him mad. In his despair, Ludovic Festergrimm stopped making toys and built . . .

something else instead. Something altogether more sinister. Something that made the people of Eerie fear him."

"What sort of something?" I ask, a second piece of fudge frozen halfway to my mouth.

"A monster," Dr. Thalassi replies, with a theatrical waggle of his eyebrows. "A giant made of bronze and clockwork. To find his lost girl and return her safely home."

"Is that the yellow face?" Violet asks. "The one painted on the sign we saw? The one with the lamp eyes and grille mouth? It looked like a robot."

"That's the one," replies the doc. "A robot. But not what you and I would expect from the word robot—this was a mechanical man built from the windup technology of two centuries ago. It would have terrified people at the time. If, that is, such a machine was ever built, which is doubtful."

"So, what happened?" I ask, chomping fudge excitedly and grabbing a fistful more. "With the robot and the clockwork and . . . and everything?"

A mechanical man! This already sounds like my favorite Eerie legend ever.

"It went on a rampage," Mrs. Fossil chips in. "Or so they say. It smashed right through walls like they were paper, crushing everything and everyone in its path. Once it was wound up, Festergrimm's robot couldn't be stopped."

"Something must have stopped it though," Violet points out, "in the end."

"I believe it was destroyed by the army," says the doc. "The local regiment was called in. Festergrimm and his robot were cornered up on the cliff top above Eerie and blown to smithereens. Bits of the mechanical giant and his inventor were scattered all over the town. And that was the end of them both.

"Except, this is Eerie-on-Sea—a town where legends always take on a life of their own—and the story didn't really end there. People have claimed to have unearthed bits of the smashed robot for years. Though one part was never found."

"Which part?" I ask breathlessly, the fudge glooping out between my fingers.

"The head," the doc replies. "Well, some say that a head *was* once discovered, only . . ."

"Only what?" asks Violet, as breathless as me.

"Only it wasn't the robot's head at all"—the doc's eyebrows go into overdrive as he leans in for dramatic effect—"but the head of Ludovic Festergrimm himself."

Mrs. Fossil's teacup rattles on its saucer.

"Oh, why do we have to talk about this?" she demands. "Trust Sebastian Eels to bring up these horrid stories again, just when we'd all forgotten them."

"And that dusty old building out there is really the place?"

says Violet, with wondering eyes. "The place where such a fan-tastic legend started?"

"It is," says Dr. Thalassi, as he helps himself to a cube of rum fudge. He inspects it like a curious artifact before popping it in his mouth. "And parts of the story must be true, at least. There really was a man named Ludovic Festergrimm who made clockwork toys there, long ago. And the army really was called in to end a disturbance, though I expect it was probably just an argument about the price of fish, rather than an attack by a killer robot. And there *are* some peculiar pieces of clockwork dotted around the town to this day. I myself have often wondered if there is a little of Festergrimm's workings in the mermonkey, for example. But you must come along to the museum one day, both of you, if you want to find out more."

"I want to know more right now!" I cry. "More about the robot. Just imagine it!"

The doc smiles.

"It's just as well you have a good imagination, Herbie, since there's nothing left of the machine these days, if indeed it did once exist. It's my belief that people have muddled the details over the years and confused the clockwork *maker* with the machine he built, until Festergrimm has become remembered as the name of the monster, not the man. But whatever the truth of it, the workshop lay empty for many years until someone had the bright idea to open a waxworks gallery there. Though even that, as you've seen, is history now."

"Except here's Sebastian Eels," Violet says, "promising to bring the waxworks back to life."

"I admit," Dr. Thalassi replies, with reluctance in his voice, "to being a little jealous of that idea. If only I had known there were so many of the figures left, I might have asked Lady Kraken to take it on myself."

"Well, I wish no one had had the idea at all!" Mrs. Fossil declares. "Some things are best forgotten."

Before we can say anything more, a customer comes in, and Mrs. F bustles over to talk to them about driftwood and shells.

"Maybe you *can* be the one to reopen it," says Vi to the doc, lowering her voice. "Why should a good idea be left to a bad man like Sebastian Eels?"

The doc places his empty teacup down and sighs as he gets to his feet.

"Don't tempt me! But the mermonkey has spoken, and I promised Jenny that Eels was to be given a second chance, and that's that. I'm not sure how I or anyone else could stop him now anyway."

"Unless we catch him up to no good," Violet replies, with a gleam in her eye. "Unless we catch him doing some *new* villainy."

"You won't catch him doing anything, Violet Parma," the doc

says, suddenly serious. "Sebastian Eels is dangerous and unpredictable. Just as he is forbidden to go near you, you and Herbie are to keep well away from him. Is that understood?"

"But—" Violet begins.

"But nothing. And don't go getting any ideas about exploring the waxworks gallery on your own," the doc adds, pulling the brass key from his pocket and waggling it at us. "Since Wendy doesn't want to be caretaker, I'll do it. If anyone is going to catch Sebastian Eels up to no good, it will be me."

And with this, he slides the key back into his pocket and leaves the Flotsamporium.

"So much for sneaking the key out of its hiding place later," says Violet, glaring at the closing shop door. "But at least it makes it easier to decide what to do next."

"Eat more fudge?" I say.

"No!" Violet grabs her coat. "I never made that promise to Jenny about giving Sebastian Eels a second chance, Herbie, and neither did you. Besides, we don't need to break into Festergrimm's to find out what Eels is up to."

"We don't?"

"Of course not." Violet pulls me to my feet and waves goodbye to Mrs. Fossil. "Because he's staying at the hotel. *Your* hotel. That means you can find out which room he's staying in, so we can break into that instead."

CHAPTER 11

ADVANCING CRABWISE

When we get back to the hotel, Violet nips behind the large metal dustbin that now lives permanently in front of my cellar window and lets herself in. I wonder if—now that she realizes Lady Kraken knows about it—Violet feels a bit disappointed that her secret way in is secret no longer. If so, she doesn't show it. And besides, it's still easier than sneaking her around the front. As for me, I stroll up the steps to the main door and try to look as cool as a cucumber (though hopefully not quite so green) as I enter the hotel the conventional way.

"How am I supposed to find out Eels's room number?" I mutter as I think over Violet's words.

"You could always ask Amber," I mutter to myself in reply. "She's Team Herbie, after all."

But before I can slide across the lobby to the reception desk and turn on the Herbie charm, I see something that stops me, and my muttering, in our tracks.

Sebastian Eels is already there! In the hotel lobby, leaning on the reception desk like he owns the place, chatting to Amber Griss, the receptionist.

And Amber is smiling.

As I watch in stunned disbelief, Eels leans forward to say something particularly secret and Amber looks away, tucking a strand of hair behind her ear.

And *giggling*!

I clutch my cap.

Making Amber smile is *my* job! I've been doing it for years.

But, just as I'm about to march over there, the annoying voice of Mr. Mollusc reaches my ear like a slap with a wet fish.

"There you are, Mr. Lemon," he says, emerging from the dining room. "Come along now, it's time you were on duty. There are lost things to take care of."

This is much more polite than the way Mollusc usually speaks to me, but the reason for that is soon apparent: behind the hotel manager are a couple of guests, also heading my way.

"Ah, there's the lad," says one of these guests. He has a

pointed mustache and is dressed in mostly tweed. He looks like the kind of man who is always wearing a uniform, even when he isn't. "Still Lost-and-Founder, eh? Finding things, and returning things, and so forth?"

"Hello, Herbie," says the other guest cheerfully. She is shorter than the man, but no less tweedy. "Remember us? We stayed here last winter."

I do a grin, one of my best, and straighten my cap. Of course I remember them. This is Colonel and Mrs. Crabwise, who stay in the hotel *every* winter. And every year they lose something and need to call me in. If you flick through the ledger—the big leather-bound book where I register all the lost items—their names appear more than most. But I don't mind. It's usually fairly straightforward finding the colonel's reading glasses where they have fallen in the jelly (true story), or Mrs. Crabwise's tennis sock where it has *ping*ed onto the roof of a fisherman's hut (don't ask!). Everyone is entitled to be something, and the something the Crabwises are is "forgetful." They always give me a nice tip at the end of their stay, which I'm sure Mr. Mollusc enjoys spending.

"Welcome back to the Grand Nautilus Hotel," I say. "Please don't hesitate to ring my bell when, I mean, *if* you need any lost-and-foundering done."

"That's just it," says Mr. Mollusc in the breezy manner he uses in front of guests. "They *have* been ringing your bell, Mr. Lemon. For some time. It seems you haven't been at your post."

And the breezy manner blows away briefly to reveal just how much trouble I'm in.

I keep the grin going, but I do a gulp at the same time, which isn't easy (try it and see!).

"Have you . . ." I ask the guests, "have you lost something, then?"

"Ah, not *lost*," says Colonel Crabwise. "Found. Thought you should take charge of it, lad. Before you call in the police."

"The police?" Mr. Mollusc and I say at exactly the same time.

"Oh, yes," replies Mrs. Crabwise. "It will certainly be a matter for the authorities."

"Um," I say, as Mr. Mollusc struggles to keep his composure. By now we're causing a bit of a stir in the lobby, and—I'm dismayed to see—Sebastian Eels is watching us from his position by the desk. He leans over and says something else to Amber, and she suppresses yet another giggle. "What," I continue, quickly, "*exactly*, have you found?"

"A ring," Mrs. Crabwise explains. "A golden ring, with a large jewel in it."

"Really?" Mr. Mollusc blinks, the light of alarm in his eyes switching to the glow of avarice. "A *golden* ring, you say? And a *jewel*? You know, perhaps I should take it into safekeeping myself . . ."

"Yes, perhaps that would be best," Mrs. Crabwise agrees. "After all, it probably isn't right to expose young Herbie to something so gruesome."

"Gruesome?" Mr. Mollusc frowns. "What's gruesome about a ring?"

"Oh, nothing," says the colonel. "It's the severed finger the ring is on that's the gruesome part."

✿O✿

Despite his obvious horror at this revelation, there's no way Mr. Mollusc can send me to deal with the ring now, not without looking like a terrible human being in front of two prized and regular guests. But I tag along anyway, and the four of us enter the gleaming elevator and head up to where the colonel and Mrs. Crabwise have made their grisly discovery.

"Do you find many fingers, Herbie?" Mrs. Crabwise asks me as we ascend. "Or is it mostly people reporting fingers missing? It must be quite distressing for one as young as you."

"Nonsense!" declares the colonel. "Herbie can take it, can't you, lad? He's a proper Lost-and-Founder. Old school. Dependable. Brass buttons always shiny. Reminds me of myself as a youngster."

"Thanks," I say, beaming, "but I'll leave this one to my manager." Then I add, to Mr. Mollusc, "You should probably use your handkerchief, sir. When you pick up the chopped finger?

You don't want to get blood and all that under your fingernails."

Mr. Mollusc glares fury at me but says nothing.

Then we arrive on the fourth floor.

"It's on the carpet, in the corridor," Mrs. Crabwise explains, leading the way. "I almost stepped on it. Ah, there it is—look!"

Sure enough, lying beside the baseboard, as if it had rolled there, is a severed finger, wearing a large golden ring with a ruby-red stone in it.

"You see?" says Colonel Crabwise. "Grim, eh? Been chopped off some time, too, I'd say, judging by the color. Seen it all before, of course. In the war. Fingers flying in all directions. Thumbs, too. Anyway, best get it bagged up, lad. Someone'll be missing that."

Mr. Mollusc, who I'm sure had been earnestly hoping this was all just a big misunderstanding, goes an even sicklier color than the finger and clutches a nearby curtain. But then, suddenly, I realize something.

I crouch down on the carpet and examine the finger. It is indeed a strange color, but something about that color seems familiar. Slowly, I reach out and give the digit a prod. It's a bit squishy, in a flubbery way I've felt before.

I pick up the severed finger and hold it up for the others to see.

Mr. Mollusc looks like he's going to faint.

"Is this your room?" I ask the colonel and Mrs. Crabwise, using the finger to point at the nearest door

"That's right," the colonel replies. "Our usual sea view."

"So," I ask, waving the finger at the door opposite, "who is staying here?"

"I am," says a voice.

Quickly I hide the finger behind my back.

Sebastian Eels, almost as if he had been following us, strides down the corridor. His face is full of polite interest, but his eyes contain a gleam of suspicion just for me.

"Is there something I can help you with, Mollusc?" Eels demands in a dangerously quiet voice.

The hotel manager gives a frightened shake of his head.

"Then I would like to be left undisturbed," says Sebastian Eels.

He rummages a key from his jacket pocket and lets himself into his room. But not before I spot something else in that pocket, something that Eels shoves back down hastily. Something I'm sure only I noticed.

It's a hand.

Someone *else's* hand.

With the index finger missing.

CHAPTER 12

A FISHY FINGER AND CHIPS

ere, catch!" I say, as I enter my Lost-and-Foundery a few minutes later and toss the severed finger to Violet.

"Herbie, where have you . . . ?" Violet starts to reply, catching the finger automatically.

Then she sees what it is.

"Ugh, *what*?" she cries, and the finger flies out of her hand. It bounces across the floor before coming to rest beside my little wood-burning stove, which is roaring merrily.

"Careful!" I say, darting forward to pick it up. "Don't want it to melt."

"Herbie!" Violet looks horrified at the object in my hand. "What is that?"

"A finger," I explain, reaching up and using it to straighten my cap, "a *waxwork* finger. It was upstairs in one of the hotel corridors, causing quite a stir just outside Sebastian Eels's room."

"Waxwork?" Violet says, relieved, as I toss the finger back to her. And I can't help grinning. It's not often that I get to rattle Violet Parma. I'm tempted to keep the finger as a trophy. Then Violet adds, "Wait, you already know which room Eels is staying in?"

"Yup," I say, puffing out my buttons and leaning casually against my repair desk as if I own the place (which I kind of do). "We Lost-and-Founders don't waste any time. Once we start working on a case, we jump right to it, and—"

"So, this finger," Violet interrupts, ignoring the lean and the buttons, "means Sebastian Eels hasn't wasted any time, either. And the mystery deepens."

"Um?" I ask, as the buttons sag. "Does it?"

"Of course!" Violet replies. "This finger means Eels must have already visited the waxworks gallery, even though he's only been in town a few hours."

"Well, yes . . ."

"And yet," says Vi, "it was pretty obvious when we went to Festergrimm's earlier that no one had been in there for years. We could hardly open the door, there was so much rubbish behind it. And I'm pretty sure no one else knew that Mrs. Fossil kept the key on a beam outside her shop. So, how does Eels have bits of wax-work on him already, if he hasn't been in through the front door?"

"Maybe," I say, "maybe there's a *back* door."

"There's a lot more to Festergrimm's than we've seen, Herbie," Violet replies, waggling the finger so that the painted metal ring and costume-glass gemstone catch the light. "Who knows how far the underground part extends. Eels probably knows more about that place than anyone. And that makes me nervous. That should make *everyone* nervous."

And I can't argue with that, can I?

"Anyway," Violet says, handing the finger back, "what happened when you confronted Sebastian Eels with this? Did Mr. Mollusc do anything? How did the other guests react?"

"I, er, I didn't quite manage to do any confronting," I admit. "And Mollusc won't do anything," I add. "He's still stuck in VIP mode when it comes to Sebastian Eels."

Violet looks cross.

"And the doc is impressed by his plans," she says, "and even Jenny wants to give him a second chance. He's winning over everyone!"

I think of Amber Griss giggling at his jokes, too, but I keep that to myself.

"He's definitely up to no good, Vi. But until we know what it is, I don't see what we can do. Except . . ."

"Yes, Herbie?"

"Except head over to Seegol's for chips and chew it all over."

And that's a plan we can both agree on.

⚙❀

We climb out the window, then hurry down the steps to the pier. It's late afternoon now, and definitely fish-and-chips o'clock if, like me and Vi, you only had fudge for lunch.

The sea crashes on either side as we walk along the pier and approach the cheery lights of Seegol's Diner, bright and welcoming against the dark of the ocean beyond. The sun, which has looked like it could hardly be bothered all day, is already sloping down toward the horizon, smearing bloodred across the sky as if planning a hasty getaway and getting its excuses in early.

Above, a single seabird tracks us in the wind.

"I hope that isn't who I think it is," says Vi.

We hurry on until we push open the door to Seegol's and enter the steamy warmth inside.

"Old friends!" calls Mr. Seegol from his scrubbed steel kitchen island in the center of the diner. Spread around him, like boats at anchor, are a dozen tables and chairs. A few early customers are already digging in to golden fried fish and chips and drinking cups of strong tea.

"Well, not so *old*," Seegol adds with a chuckle, as he heads over to us, "but definitely *friends*. What will I bring you? Are you here to celebrate?"

"Celebrate, Mr. Seegol?" Violet asks.

"Ah, but perhaps you haven't heard . . ." Seegol is beaming as he leads us to a table, clearly delighted to be the one giving us news for a change. "The old waxworks gallery is reopening. It will bring more visitors, and more visitors means more fish and chips. Everyone is talking about it."

But when Mr. Seegol sees the looks on our faces, his smile dissolves.

"You don't like?" he says. "Maybe waxworks is scary for you?"

"*Everyone* is talking about it?" says Vi, as we sit. "Really?"

"My customers have been," Seegol replies. "All day! But it is not good news for you, I see that. So, what can I bring to make you happy? And, Herbie," he adds, turning an inquiring eyebrow on to me, "what have you brought for me?"

I rummage in my pockets, pulling out a handful of stuff. I spill it across the table, including the recently acquired waxwork digit. If Mr. Seegol is fazed by the sight of a chopped-off finger rolling between the salt and pepper shakers, he doesn't show it. "Anything good here, Mr. Seegol?" I ask. "Good enough for a couple of bowls of chips, and maybe some onion rings?"

Seegol pokes about among the pocket treasures, then

selects a gold tie pin. It has been in my Lost-and-Foundery—unclaimed—for over a hundred years, which means it's mine now, according to the rules.

"For this, I bring you the works," he says, "with extras!"

"I can't believe it," Violet whispers, as Seegol heads back to his kitchen. "The whole town seems to know about Eels's plan already!"

"You know what Eerie-on-Sea is like." I shrug. "Gossip travels faster than the tide."

"If only the doc hadn't taken that key." Violet bangs the table with her fist, making my pocket things jump. "We need to get back into Festergrimm's!"

"What happened to breaking into Eels's hotel room?" I ask after a pause during which the first round of chips arrive, filling our noses with vinegary steam.

"We can't very well do that when he's there, can we?" Vi replies, chomping a chip. "But if he's there that means the waxworks gallery will be empty right now. Even Sebastian Eels can't be in two places at once. So, *that* means—"

But I don't get to hear what that means because there is a sudden *RAT-AT-AT* on the window, right beside our table. We jump, startled, to find that Bagfoot the Eerie-on-Seagull is perched on the sill just outside!

He raps again on the glass with his beak.

"Unbelievable!" I cry, nearly choking on a chip at seeing the bird so close. But just as I raise a fist to bang on the window myself and frighten the pesky fudge thief away, I see that the seagull's beady yellow eye is fixed not on our bowls but on something else on the table beyond them.

Slowly, Vi and I turn our heads to see what could possibly be more fascinating to a hungry seagull than chips.

And it's the finger.

The severed *waxwork* finger.

Which has begun to move!

CHAPTER 13

UPS AND DOWNS

With a sickening creak, the chopped-off waxwork finger caterpillar-flexes—once, twice—as it crawls across our table like a putrid worm.

Toward me!

Then, as suddenly as it started, the revolting thing quivers to a stop, falls slowly onto its side, and goes still.

"Did you see that?" I manage to gasp, though the shock on Vi's face is answer enough.

"Hey! Get away! Go on, please, *shoo*!" cries Mr. Seegol, rushing toward us, basket of onion rings in one hand, waving at the seagull with the other. Bagfoot, with a final glance at the finger, shrieks, opens his wings, and reluctantly flies off.

"Cheeky bird!" says Mr. Seegol with an apologetic grin as he puts the basket in front of us. Then he goes outside to wave a tea towel at the sky and dance about, in case any of Bagfoot's pals get any ideas about bothering his customers. It would probably be quite funny to watch, but Vi and I can't take our eyes off the flubbery digit on the table. After a moment, Violet reaches out with her fork and jabs at it.

Nothing happens.

"Maybe . . ." she says, "maybe it was the motion of the waves under the pier . . . ?"

"I told you earlier that I saw a waxwork move!" I hiss under my breath. "Now we've both seen it."

Violet twitches her nose in thought.

Then, gingerly, she picks up the finger.

"Careful!" I squeak as she holds the chopped end close to her face and squints at it. Then she bends the horrible thing back and forth with a metallic squeak.

". . . hear that?" she says. "Metal joints. What if the wax-works are *supposed* to move, Herbie? Like . . . like robots."

"Robots?"

"I bet there are gears and levers in all those waxwork figures," Violet says, tossing the finger over to me. "And clockwork."

I peer at the finger, and sure enough—visible in the wax like bone within a real chopped digit—there is the tip of a brass rod and ends of rusty wires.

"But, Vi . . ."

"We're getting scared over nothing," Violet declares. "Just a bunch of wax-covered mechanisms."

"Yes, but, *Vi* . . ."

"No, Herbie." Violet grabs a couple of onion rings as if the discussion is over. "You of all people should know better. You're a clockwork expert!"

An expert? Well, I like hearing that, even though it's not really true. But I do know enough about clockwork and levers and gears to understand one important thing: they only move if something—usually a spring—is driving them. And, as I look again at the finger in my hand, I know for certain that there is no room for a spring inside it. And therefore, even if Violet's right, there's still no way this finger should have moved on its own.

I put it down quickly.

"Anyway, this settles it," Violet continues, ignoring my silence. "Eat up, Herbie! We're breaking into Festergrimm's tonight."

✿⚙✿

A little while later, under cover of evening, Vi and I are lurking in the shadow of a doorway in Fargazi Round. We see lights on deep in Mrs. Fossil's Flotsamporium, but the building we've come for—in the very middle of the square—is completely dark. As the first stars twinkle above us, Festergrimm's Eerie Waxworks is as closed and silent as the grave.

"There isn't a loose board anywhere!" Violet whispers in frustration, after we've circled the place several times and tugged and tapped at every plank and window. "No way to squeeze in at all."

I pop a chip into my mouth and give it a thoughtful chomp. Violet was so keen to get here that I asked Mr. Seegol to put the rest of our chips in a cardboard cone to bring with us.

"If you were planning some squeezing in, Vi," I say, "we should have done that before chips, not after."

"Did you have to bring those?" Violet asks.

"I eat when I'm nervous," I explain, offering her the cone. She shakes her head. "Which is, I admit, a lot of the time."

"Well, once you've finished being nervous," Vi asks, "do think you can pick the lock?"

"Not without Clermit's help," I reply. "And it's a bit late to go collect him from the doc now. Anyway, he's broken, remember? And the doc said he couldn't fix him."

I know from previous adventures that Clermit has a Swiss army knife's worth of tools inside him, as well as a fabulous mechanism, and more mysteries besides. I'm not surprised that even Dr. Thalassi can't put him back together again.

"Perhaps we should get a hammer and just smash our way in," Violet says, sounding like she's only half joking. "We have to get down to that underground gallery somehow, Herbie!"

"Some get down to business," agrees a feline voice from the shadows, "while others get *up* to no good."

There's movement above, and we look up to the roof of Festergrimm's to see a white whiskery face peering down at us with ice-blue eyes.

"Erwin!" Violet cries in delight. "So, which are you doing?"

"Up to no good, I'd say," I reply, as the cat begins licking his paws like he's no different from any other cat in the world. "I have a horrible feeling he wants us to join him on the roof."

"The roof!" Violet says. "Of course."

Now that he has our attention, Erwin slinks along the rickety metal gutter until he reaches one of two small dormer windows poking out of the roof tiles. These aren't boarded up, and one in particular seems tumbledown from storm damage.

"Herbie, give me a boost up," says Violet.

"Seriously?" I reply, nearly choking on a chip.

"Yes, seriously. Help me up, and I'll pull you after me."

So, with the cone of chips clamped in my teeth, I make a foothold with my hands and propel Violet upward. She grips the gutter and scampers up onto the roof. Then she leans back down toward me.

"Come on, Herbie," she whispers. "Use the drainpipe to reach my hand."

So, with the chips still dangling, I pull myself up the drainpipe and reach one trembly hand for Violet's.

And it's then, at the moment of maximum inconvenience, that the seagull strikes.

Bagfoot, who must have been watching us from some unseen perch, swoops at me—filling my face with shrieks and flapping whiteness—and seizes my cone of chips in his huge yellow beak.

"Geroff!" I shout, probably louder than I should, given that we're breaking and entering private property, and my hand slips from Violet's. With my weight suddenly gone, Vi flies backward and bashes through the rickety dormer window. I hear her cry out as she falls with a tremendous crash somewhere inside Festergrimm's Eerie Waxworks.

"Violet!" I shout at the top of my whisper. "Vi! Can you hear me?"

Nothing but silence answers from inside the building. Bagfoot, with a cry of triumph, lands in the square. Two other seagulls join him, and the three of them start tearing the cone of chips to pieces.

CHAPTER 14

TRITONS AND MERROWS AND BLUE MEN FROM LEGEND

There's a rule of lost-and-foundering that says if something takes a turn for the worse, it can always be turned back around again for the better. The rule doesn't say *how* this can be done—that would be too easy—but just knowing it's possible is encouraging. So that's why the first thing I do when I pick myself up is rush to the building and cry, "Well done, Vi—you're in!" as if her falling was all part of the plan.

But then I add, as I hear a moan from inside, "I'm coming!"

I grab the drainpipe and pull myself up with a few desperate scrabbles of my feet. I heave myself onto the roof tiles and shine my flashlight down through the broken window.

Below me, lying sprawled in a tangle with one of the wax-works, lies my friend Violet Parma.

I dangle myself down through the window, and then drop with an "Argh!" as I fall, and an "Ooph!" when I land. I'm relieved to see Violet raise herself on one elbow as Erwin licks her face in concern.

"Anything broken?" I ask, thinking this would be a great moment for a "nope!"

"Just an arm," Violet replies, tugging a horribly bent wax-work limb from beneath her and waving it in the air. The hand flops limply from side to side.

"What have I done, Herbie," she adds, as she gets to her feet, "to make an enemy of that seagull?"

"No idea," I say, clicking on my flashlight again and shin-ing it around, "but it's me he keeps stealing from. Hey, puss!" I continue, turning to Erwin. "Where were you when the air raid happened? Aren't cats supposed to catch birds?"

"Psstht!" goes Erwin in reply, flattening his ears and sticking his tongue out.

"Stop waving the flashlight around, Herbie," Violet says, steadying my arm. "Look!"

The interior of the waxworks museum, picked out in the narrow flashlight beam of swirling dust motes, is even more unnerving at night than it was in the day. The distorted, waxy face of Saint Dismal leers insanely at us, while Purple Pimm, the fearsome lady pirate, looms over me, her cutlass raised. Other figures, still shrouded in white cloth, stand motionless and strange. In the small light and eerie atmosphere, it's like being surrounded by ghosts.

"Well, at least we're in," Violet whispers.

"Yes," I reply, as we back up against the shop counter and cobwebby souvenir stand, "but now I'm wondering how we're going to get out again. I can't see any way to climb back up to that window."

The old Festergrimm's sign is leaning where we left it, the robot head staring blankly at us from the middle. It doesn't look as impressive close up, I guess, as it would from afar. I give the head a knock with my knuckles, and it makes a dull, wooden sound.

"I wonder what happened to the real thing," I say, remembering what Dr. Thalassi told us of the legend and of the head of the robot that was never found.

"If there is another way in and out of this place," Violet says, ignoring my question, "we'll probably find it downstairs."

"Except there aren't any stairs," I say. "The only way down appears to be in that." And I point to the train of antique carriages on its track.

Together we approach the train. Erwin jumps in and searches

all around, as cats do when they go somewhere new. All three carriages are blanketed with dust and bat droppings and don't look like they've been used for decades.

"I wonder how fast it goes," says Violet.

"I am NOT riding this train," I declare. "And neither are you. It's because of moments like this that I was doing Nope-vember in the first place."

"I'm not sure it would go now anyway." Violet tugs at a carriage, but it stays completely immobile on the track. "It probably needs electricity. But at least that means it'll be safe to explore the tunnel without having the train roll down behind us. Come on, Herbie—you have the only flashlight, so you can go first."

I don't reply. I suddenly can't stop staring at something behind us.

"Herbie?"

I'm shining the flashlight on the figure of Captain Pimm.

"She's . . ." I say with a gulp, "she's *moved.*"

"Stop it, Herbie." Violet sounds annoyed. "This is no time for jokes."

"I'm serious," I reply. "She was facing the door when we came in. Now she's looking right at *us!*"

In the flashlight beam the pirate grins, still as bones.

"Well, she's not moving now," says Violet, almost managing to keep the tremble out of her voice. "Maybe I bumped her, or something, when I fell. Come on—we need to find a clue before this place drives us mad with fright."

And so, keeping close together—and with me still throwing anxious glances over my shoulder at the waxwork pirate—we edge into the tunnel and descend the first few rungs of train track. Then we part the tattered black curtain.

The fisherman waxwork that terrified me earlier is just where I left him, still staring our way. I feel an even greater rush of unease at the sight of his ghastly face and grasping hands.

"Clockwork, Herbie," Violet whispers beside me. "Remember that. It's all just machines and clockwork."

Her words are not quite as reassuring as they should be, but I tell myself she must be right. When we draw level with the fisherman, I give him a friendly pat on the shoulder. His mouth falls open with a cloud of dust and dead spiders, so I hurry on.

We continue to pick our way down the tracks, around a slow bend in the tunnel. New waxworks appear: a gruesome mermaid with tangled hair and little pointed teeth, who is frozen mid-bite as she takes the head off a fish; a diver in an old-fashioned diving costume and brass helmet, who is battling with a harpoon against a giant tentacle; a sea captain from a different age than Purple Pimm, who is leaning on the rail of an iron battleship, looking through a telescope at something farther down the tunnel.

"Is that . . . is that Captain Kraken?" I gasp, recognizing the figure from our previous adventures, despite the horribly unnatural hue of the wax.

"If it is," says Violet, "then that could mean he's looking at—"

"The malamander!" I cry out, as I shine the flashlight farther on.

The famous monster of Eerie-on-Sea spans the whole tunnel here, glowering over the tracks, his terrible mouth filled with tooth needles and his back bristling with spines.

"But not," says Vi, tapping the creature's papier-mâché scales, "anywhere near as scary as the real thing. He must be here to guard the main gallery. Look, Herbie—the tunnel is coming to an end."

As we creep gingerly beneath the scaly underbelly of the malamander, the tunnel is indeed opening out into a cavernous underground space. I swing the flashlight from side to side to take it all in.

Stalactites and crystal-rock formations provide a backdrop for more ghastly waxwork figures, which hang and snarl and grasp toward where the train would pass. Tritons, merrows, and Blue Men from legend vie with pirates and rum smugglers and some of the scariest mermaids I've ever seen. But the strange magic of the place is spoiled by the fusty air of neglect and decay, and the cobwebs that cover it all.

"The track runs past all the exhibits," Violet says. "And you know, creepy as it is, I would have *loved* to ride that train back when Festergrimm's was open. Wouldn't you?"

Despite my queasy feelings, a tiny bit of me agrees with Violet. This place is amazing.

"I just can't believe I didn't know it existed," I say. "Maybe . . ."

"Yes?" Violet turns to me. "Maybe what?"

"Maybe"—I look down and fiddle with my buttons—"just *maybe* . . . Sebastian Eels really *is* on to something good here. Reopening the waxworks, I mean."

"Herbie!" Violet is outraged. "Not you, too!"

"I'm just saying," I answer, as quickly as I can, "that I can't really see what mischief he can do by reopening this place. It's just a moldy old waxworks museum full of broken-down models, and . . ."

We hear a sound.

A loud bang from somewhere deep in the basement gallery.

"What's that?" Violet gasps. "Did you hear it?"

Well, of course I did. And now, as we turn the flashlight beam this way and that, we hear another thud. And then a metallic clang. And *then*, carrying on the stale air of this underground freak show, we hear the moaning of a human voice.

CHAPTER 15

THINGS IN JARS

ime to go!" I whisper, putting my feet into reverse, but
Violet grabs my arm.

"Nope!" she whispers back. "Not before we find out
more. Come on!"

She takes my flashlight, hides most of its beam in the sleeve
of her too-big coat, and creeps forward past the terrifying waxwork figure of a trident-wielding merman. Erwin is on Violet's
shoulders now, his tail swishing in alarm.

I tiptoe after them, hardly whimpering at all. We pass several more eerie waxwork dioramas I don't like to look at too
closely, and then come to a halt.

Just as in all ghost train tunnels, the walls of this underground space are painted black, but ahead there is a sliver of light, as if a secret door is slightly open. By the time I get there, Violet already has her eye pressed up to the crack and is peering in.

"What can you see?" I hiss.

"A corridor," she replies, "with another door at the end."

There come further banging sounds from beyond that second door, and then a brief *whoosh* like the jet of a blowtorch, before a voice says, "Now then, madam. This won't hurt a bit . . ."

Then there's a shriek, as if a power saw is slicing through something hard.

Like bone.

Now, at this point, most people would turn around and run away. And I *want* to run away, I really do. But most people don't have a best friend like Violet, and what Violet does next stops my running away in its tracks.

Violet opens the black door, steps stealthily into the dimly lit corridor . . .

and tiptoes *toward* the gruesome sounds!

"There, my pretty!" comes the voice again, from behind the second door. "And now, let's see what's inside your skull . . ."

The power tool starts up again.

Violet reaches the second door and puts her eye to the crack, just as before. I do the same and witness a scene of horror that I don't think I will ever forget.

Sebastian Eels is standing at a table in the middle of a room full of body parts. Torsos hang from hooks in the ceiling, heads loll about on shelves, and legs and arms are heaped crazily in baskets.

There is a whole display case full of just eyeballs.

There are . . . *things* . . . in jars.

It looks like a cross between an engineer's workshop and Dr. Frankenstein's laboratory.

Eels himself is dressed in a smeary leather apron, long leather gloves, and tinted goggles. In one hand he holds an angle grinder—a power tool for cutting through metal—while he uses the other to hold down a body on the table.

Yes, a body!

There's a roar from the power tool, and sparks fly out in a blaze of light as Eels cuts through. Then, after a *pang* of breaking metal, Eels raises the severed head of his victim—some kind of hideous sea witch, by the looks of her—high in his hand. He peers into the gaping neck.

"Pah!" he snorts into the cavity. "Nothing? Well, you'll pay for disappointing me . . ."

Then he picks up a blowtorch and, with a roar of flame, turns it on the head. The melting, flubbery face of the waxwork sea witch slides off onto the table, revealing an iron skull beneath.

Eels turns the skull in his hand, so he can get a screwdriver into its ear for a closer look inside. One of the sea witch's eyes falls out and rolls across the floor toward us.

"Damn it!" Eels spits in irritation, slamming the head down into the wreckage of the body. "But it's here somewhere, it must be. I'll find it, even if I have to melt down the whole stinking lot of them."

And he wipes sweat from his brow, leaving a smear of wax-work gore on his forehead, before dragging another victim—this time a medieval sailor—over to his butcher's table.

Violet pulls her head back from the door and looks at me with terrified eyes.

"I knew it!" she gasps.

"It's a massacre!" I agree.

"No, I mean he isn't fixing anything," Violet adds. "He's *looking* for something."

"Then we can go now," I squeak, as the shriek of power tools starts up again.

"Not yet," Violet says. "He's talking to himself—maybe we can find out more."

And so, we put our eyes back to the crack, and see . . .

. . . that Sebastian Eels is right there! Behind the door! Looking back at us through the smoky lenses of his goggles!

We jump back, but it's too late—Eels bangs the door open, knocking us to the ground. He steps out and towers over us, the angle grinder spinning in one hand, while the blowtorch spits a jet of fire from the other.

"You two!" he declares. "I might have known."

We scrabble desperately to our feet and run back along the corridor. When we reach the second door, Violet skids around and slams it with a bang. But if she hoped it would somehow keep the waxworks murderer contained, she must be as dismayed as I feel when this door is kicked open, too. Eels steps out into the subterranean gallery, the fire erupting from the blowtorch reflecting in his lens-covered eyes.

"We've caught you!" Violet cries. "I knew *A Christmas Carol* didn't mean you could be trusted. You're not here to reopen Festergrimm's—you're . . . you're *up to no good*!"

"Oh, really?" Eels says, revving the angle grinder with a deranged grin. "And what does the great detective Violet Parma and her sad little lost-and-foundling think I'm up to exactly?"

"You're . . . you're looking for something!" Violet shoots back. "We heard you. And I bet it's . . . it's *something you shouldn't have.*"

Sebastian Eels's grin turns sour at these words, and he jumps forward, thrusting the angle grinder at us. The machine roars, but then powers down as—back in the workshop—the plug comes out of the wall. Eels flings it away in disgust, but he still has his blowtorch.

"You know nothing!" he says. "And what's it to you, anyway? Why are you two *always* poking your noses into my business? Why are you even in here?"

He circles around, as if trying to herd us in a particular direction, pulsing flame from his blowtorch the whole time.

"But, of course," he adds, "I already know the answer. You,

Violet, are your father's daughter, after all. Poor lost Peter Parma was always interfering in my affairs, and you're even worse."

"Don't talk about my dad!" Violet yells, and I have to hold her back. "It's your fault I lost him. And my mum! It's because of you they disappeared."

"Aw, diddums." Eels tips his head to one side, in mock sympathy. "But perhaps I can help. I promised Lady Kraken I'd make some new waxworks, and Peter was surely one of the most famous people in the history of Eerie-on-Sea. I can make a likeness of him, Violet, for you to visit and cry over."

And with these words, Sebastian Eels pushes his flame against the face of a nearby waxwork smuggler. The smuggler's eyes, nose, and mouth sag in the heat, so Eels roughly reshapes them into a grotesque new face.

"There!" He chuckles. "Looks just like your dad. Ha!"

"You're a monster!" Violet cries, almost breaking free from my grip, though what she thinks she can do against a deranged author armed with fire, I don't know. But my mind is already racing, zooming back over everything we've seen and done so far. I think of the story the doc told us about old Festergrimm and his robot, and about how it was blown to smithereens. I think about the clockwork bits and mechanisms that seem to be hidden in the waxwork models.

"I know what you're looking for," I say, surprising even myself with how sure I sound. "You're looking for Festergrimm's robot."

Then I add, my mind leaping back to all the things we've ever heard Eels say to us in our previous adventures.

"You're looking for Festergrimm's robot, because . . . because you think it can help you find *the deepest secret of Eerie-on-Sea!*"

There's a moment of silence following my words. Eels looks shocked, his face hollowed out in the flickering light of the blowtorch. Then his features fill with rage, and I know that I have hit this particular nail squarely on the head.

"You think you're so smart, don't you?" Eels says in a voice full of menace. "You think you know *all* about it."

"Um . . ." I start to say, because actually, *no, I don't.* The deepest secret of Eerie-on-Sea is something we've heard Eels mention again and again—and he once even told me I was personally connected to it in some way. But we've never been able to find out exactly what it is, or why Eels is so determined to find it.

Violet and I keep retreating, looking around for the tunnel that brought us here. In the shock of the moment, we have gotten ourselves completely disoriented.

"And I suppose you know all about mad old Festergrimm, too?" Eels asks, advancing toward us again, driving us ever farther into a corner. "And his vengeful robot?"

A white shape moves in the dark behind Eels. It's Erwin,

looking at us with "follow me!" eyes. He runs off into the dark, darting between the waxworks, and suddenly I see the mouth of the tunnel. Erwin turns when he reaches the entrance, blinking at us to hurry.

"But I don't need to find Festergrimm's robot, Herbert Lemon," Eels continues, stepping onto the train tracks and reaching out to a large shape nearby—a large shape covered in a white dust sheet. "I don't need to find him, because . . . *he's right here!*"

And with this, he pulls the cloth down to reveal something amazing and terrifying.

CHAPTER 16

EELS THE IMPALER

he robot!" I whisper.

Despite everything, this is a whisper of wonder rather than fear, because standing before us—at the heart of the waxworks gallery—is a giant man made of bronze. His eyes are lamps above a metal-grille mouth. His shoulders are broader than a bus. Two mighty arms are poised at his side, as if ready to crush and smash and destroy.

"You are *wrong*, Herbert Lemon," Eels declares, "with your little theories. For behold, I already have the mighty Festergrimm's robot at my side. And now—"

Without warning, the man darts forward, spitting fire and making a grab for us, but I dive one way, and Violet goes the other.

"MEOW!" comes an urgent call from Erwin. Vi and I both run toward him and the safety of the tunnel.

"But the robot . . ." I gasp to Violet, as we go.

"It's not real," Violet says. And then, because of the look on my face, she adds, "It's just a model, Herbie. Like everything else here. Now, *run!*"

I turn back for moment and understand that Violet must be right. The great metal robot, which looked so powerful when it was revealed, is actually wobbling as Eels dodges around it. And I see that the bronze color is just paint.

Violet grabs me, and we run into the tunnel. But at the entrance, I look back again.

"Wait!" I say. "Where's Eels? I can't see him now."

Violet—already a few steps up the railway track in the dark of the tunnel with Erwin, turns to me impatiently. "Herbie?"

And then I spot Eels. He's beside the model of Festergrimm's robot, pulling open a small door in a column of fiberglass shaped like a stalagmite. Inside, I can just make out—in the light of the blowtorch—a few buttons on a control panel. Eels turns with a look of triumph at me as he presses a button.

The button lights up.

What's he doing? I have a sudden fear that he has activated the robot somehow—that maybe it *is* real after all. And, indeed, there is a rumbling sound from deep inside the gallery walls. But the robot doesn't move. So, what . . . ?

It's only as Violet shouts again for me to "come *on*, Herbie!" that I realize what the button does.

"Vi!" I cry, turning to look at my friend running up inside the tunnel. "Violet, the train!"

The rumble turns into a roar, and a rush of wind blows down the tunnel. Sudden light streams around the bend as the antique train hurtles toward us at high speed.

Violet scoops up Erwin and leaps desperately back down the tunnel. I grab a fistful of her coat and pull them both out of the way, just as the three carriages burst from the tunnel mouth, rolling much faster than any ghost train I've ever heard of.

Sebastian Eels growls in frustration.

He throws his blowtorch to one side, pushes the goggles up onto his forehead, and runs to the waxwork merman we saw earlier. In a moment, he has yanked the trident out of the merman's webby hands, and he throws it at us with great force.

We duck, and the trident skewers a lighthouse keeper beside us with a sickening *thunk*, as we disappear into the shadows of the gallery.

"Come out, come out, wherever you are!" Eels calls as he turns this way and that, peering into the gloom.

He can't see us, but from where we hide, we see him. He reaches back to the control panel and presses another button. All around us, the waxworks gallery comes alive with light and sound.

Eyes flash, waxwork limbs twitch, and strange and spooky sounds emerge as the entire tourist attraction flickers into eerie life. Puffs of dust and water vapor catch the light, forming a glowing, swirling mist, and we hear a terrifying ghost train wail as the carriages clatter around the twisty underground track.

"So, how do you like my little waxworks show?" Eels calls. "I just feel it needs some new exhibits. You two, perhaps? Boiled in molten wax and pinned to the wall. Heh, heh! The sign would read HERBIE AND VIOLET—THE LEGENDARY LOSERS OF EERIE-ON-SEA!"

Violet and I are behind a group of waxwork pirates now, who are standing around a large treasure chest in what appears to be a crystal cave. But I don't have time to wonder what Eerie story they depict—if we try to move again now, we'll be seen in the light of the show.

"We-ow m-ow-eow," says Erwin, who is back on Violet's shoulders. Violet nods in agreement.

"It's probably our best chance," she says.

"Ow-wow me-ow?" Erwin adds, glancing at me doubtfully, one catbrow raised.

"Yes, I'm sure Herbie's up to it," Violet tells him. "It's just matter of timing, that's all."

"Er, excuse me?" I whisper. "What's going on?"

"The train," Violet replies. "Look! It's coming back."

And she points toward the tunnel. The train, having completed a circuit, has already reemerged in the subterranean gallery and is rattling back toward us.

"We need to get on it, Herbie."

"What?" I gasp, but Violet is already moving.

"NOW!" she cries, throwing Erwin into the first carriage as the train reaches us, and then diving into the second. "Herbie!"

I have no time to speak, no time to think, barely even time to feel surprised as I clutch my Lost-and-Founder's cap and hurl myself into the third carriage. I'm barely in before I have to cling on with white knuckles as we take a bend at crazy speed.

"Why's it so fast?" I gasp.

"Eels must've dialed up the speed," Vi replies, clinging on, too. "Look out!"

Sebastian Eels appears suddenly out of the shadows and thrusts the trident—back in his hands already—straight at us. The weapon hits the carriage I'm in, glances off in a shower of sparks, and takes my Lost-and-Founder's cap with it.

"Hey!" I cry, as we hurtle past him. Then I get slapped in the face by a curtain of rubber seaweed and suddenly we're in the dark again.

"What happened?" Violet asks.

"We're in the other tunnel," I reply. "The one that goes back upstairs."

Sure enough the train begins to ascend, going slower now. Ghoulish faces leer at us in flickering electrical light, and a pirate—another of Purple Pimm's crew, I imagine—reaches toward us, out of a cloud of foul-smelling vapor. Then there is one last ghost train wail, and we emerge into the street-level room above. The train slows at the little station, opposite the counter and souvenir stand. Erwin leaps smartly off, and Violet follows.

"That's lucky . . ." I start to say, but as I put one wobbly foot out and get ready to disembark, the train suddenly speeds up again, and I fall back, sprawling on the seat.

"Herbie!" Violet shouts, reaching for me, but even as I sit up, I'm already through the tattered black curtain and gone.

Back into the tunnel!

So now I'm descending again, at crazy speed, back down into the waxworks world of Eerie-on-Sea. *And* into the waiting clutches of the diabolical Sebastian Eels and the prongs of his trident. As I see my old friend the beardy fisherman with the net loom over my head, and the horrible mermaid with her fishy dinner rush past, I try to remember how often these ghost-train-type amusement attractions usually go around. Isn't it three times? If so—and since it has been around twice already—I just have to hang on without getting spiked once more till I'm back at the station.

With a ghoulish wail, the train rolls out into the underground gallery. I see the strange lights and the eerie waxworks again, and the great model of Festergrimm's robot, standing colossally in the middle, surrounded by clouds of vapor and strobing lights. But there's no sign of Eels. Until . . .

"BOO!" he bellows, leaping from behind a sea witch's cauldron and landing in the first carriage of the train. My Lost-and-Founder's cap is still on one of the prongs of his trident. "And now," he adds, "for a game I like to call Impaling the Lemon!"

And he thrusts the trident right at me. I duck and it smashes into the seat, forcing me to the floor of the carriage as we twist and turn around the exhibits. We reenter the exit tunnel, and I can do nothing but stay down and cling on as the ghost train brings the murderous Eels back up to Violet and Erwin above.

In no time, we reach the top of the tunnel and clatter to a halt at the little station upstairs. I look up to find Eels blazing down at me in triumph, raising the trident as if to finish me off. But just then the main lights blink on. Eels freezes, still poised to strike. Slowly, he turns his head.

I don't have much else to do, so I turn my head, too.

Violet is standing beside the counter, near the souvenir stand, clutching Erwin in her arms. Beside her, his finger on the light switch, is Dr. Thalassi, holding a heavy walking stick like a club. Beside him is Mrs. Fossil, armed with a rolling pin. Several of the townsfolk are there, too, some in bathrobes, all staring in disbelief at the scene before them.

"Golly!" says Mrs. Fossil, into the silence.

CHAPTER 17

CREEPY BOOKS
AND CAT CLUES

Sebastian Eels sits back and runs his fingers through his mad hair—which, I can't help noticing, is full of flecks of melted wax. He is still wearing the gory leather apron.

"And that, dear Herbie," he says, forcing a desperate grin onto his mouth, "is just how scary Festergrimm's will be once I've finished fixing it up. Here," he adds, tugging my cap off his trident and handing it back to me, "your hat."

"What," says Dr. Thalassi, "in the name of all that is unholy, is going on here?"

"Just a little demonstration." Eels is out of the train now. "I'm sorry to say that Herbie and Violet broke into my wax-works gallery, despite the fact that it's a dangerously unsafe place to be right now." He waggles his finger at us. "Someone could get badly hurt. Really, Thalassi, I'm surprised you didn't tell them to keep away."

"I did tell them . . ." the doc protests, but before he can finish, Violet bursts in.

"He's not fixing up anything!" she cries. "He's doing terrible things to the waxworks. He's cutting them, and melting them, and . . . and . . . threatening to do the same to us!"

"No, no," Eels says, holding up the trident as if it's merely an interesting specimen and not a potential murder weapon. Dr. Thalassi's eyebrows drop into a thunderous line over his eyes, and he hefts the walking stick.

"This trident isn't *real*," Eels quickly adds. "Just a prop! You said it yourself, Violet, there's nothing real in Festergrimm's. It's just a world of waxwork illusions. But you two scallywags are proving just how great this attraction will be for the town. Think how many more tourists we'll get once I've reopened it. What a glory it will be! What a gift for Eerie-on-Sea!"

There's a murmur among the townsfolk gathered at the door. Whether or not they are excited by the prospect of more tourists, the initial alarm seems to melt away from their faces, and they begin to disperse and head back to their homes.

"But, Dr. Thalassi," Violet says. "We *saw* him. He *is* up to something, we just know it."

"Oh, humbug!" Sebastian Eels says, disagreeing with Violet, but also neatly reminding the doc and Mrs. Fossil about the book that he, Eels, was dispensed by the mermonkey. "*Bah* humbug."

Dr. Thalassi lowers his cane. But only slightly.

"Violet, Herbie," he says, "take your cat and go. This is no place for you. Wendy, take them away. I'm going to have a little word with Mr. Eels. And we're going to get a few things straight."

Mrs. Fossil steers Violet and me out into the square, while Dr. Thalassi closes the door behind us. I just have time to see the startled look on Sebastian Eels's face, as the doc turns toward him, tapping the cane against the palm of his hand.

"Are they . . . ?" Violet looks at the closed door of Festergrimm's, wide-eyed. "Are they going to *fight*?"

"Oh, no," Mrs. Fossil says, leading us to her shop. "The doc isn't really the fighting type. He won't start anything, though he could certainly *finish* it, if it came to that. But what were you two doing in there? Oh, I just *knew* that place would be trouble. Why did Festergrimm's ever have to be remembered?"

Inside the Flotsamporium, we sit beside the stove as Mrs. Fossil clatters milk onto the hot plate to make cocoa.

"And the noises that have been coming out of the place!" she continues, spooning chocolate powder into mugs. "Crashing and wailing! It reminds me of . . . Well, anyway, I called the doc to come quick with the key, but I think half the town heard it. So, what *were* you doing in there?"

I shrug. I'm not sure what, if anything, Violet and I have actually achieved by our break-in. When Mrs. Fossil brings the hot drinks over, she also brings more fudge, but my mind is too full of melted waxworks to stomach eating fudge right now.

"Do you know anything about the legend of Festergrimm, Mrs. Fossil?" Violet asks, warming her hands on her mug, while Erwin rumbles on her lap. "Apart from what the doc told us earlier? Anything about the robot that attacked the town, or the man who built it?"

"It's just an eerie tale," the beachcomber replies, "best left forgotten."

As she says this, she glances briefly at the wall.

Now, the walls of Mrs. Fossil's Flotsamporium are as jumbled as the rest of the place—with every spare surface covered by beachcombed finds and tide-rolled thingamajigs. But as I follow Mrs. F's gaze, I spot the corner of a surprisingly ornate picture frame. I've never noticed this before, but the picture it surrounds, whatever it is, is covered so nearly completely that it seems to be deliberately hidden.

"Mrs. Fossil," I say, still glancing at the concealed picture, "have you ever heard of something called the deepest secret of Eerie-on-Sea?"

Mrs. Fossil pauses her cocoa mid-slurp and locks her eyes on to mine.

"Heavens, Herbie!" she says, after a pause. "What a question! Why ever would you ask me something like that?"

"You have heard of it?" Violet asks. "Or you haven't?"

Mrs. Fossil stares into her mug, as if she might find an answer there.

"Secrets!" she says in the end, glancing again at the hidden picture on the wall. "I bet there's nowhere quite as full of those as this town. It stands to reason there must be one that's deeper than all the rest, and that's all I'll say."

"So, you can't think of any reason why Sebastian Eels would be interested in the waxworks gallery?" says Violet, also glancing at the picture. "Other than what he says?"

Mrs. Fossil manages a shrug.

"He writes creepy books," she replies. "I'm not surprised he likes creepy waxworks, too. I just wish he wasn't liking them right in front of my shop!"

"I wonder how Eels got in there," Violet continues. "There must be another way in. Do you think there might be a Netherways door beneath the waxworks gallery?"

At this, Mrs. Fossil purses her lips and takes even greater interest in the bottom of her mug. The Netherways is the name given to the vast unmapped network of tunnels, caverns, and smugglers' caves that riddle Eerie Rock, on which the town is built, like the holes in a particularly unstable Swiss cheese.

"I suppose there could be," Mrs. F agrees in the end. "They say there are secret doors in many of the cellars in Eerie, though most have been found and blocked up long since. Fancy you knowing about that, Violet! But don't go getting any crazy ideas about trying to get into them. There is a long history of people getting lost down there and never being seen again."

Violet sips her drink and says nothing. I wonder what Mrs. Fossil would say if she knew we've already used the Netherways in our past adventures. Twice!

We finish the hot chocolate, and—after a few quick good-nights and a promise that we'll go straight to bed—we leave the Flotsamporium.

Festergrimm's Eerie Waxworks stands still and dark in the middle of Fargazi Round. It seems that whatever Dr. Thalassi and his cane had to say to Sebastian Eels has already been said, and the place is as silent and locked up as it ever was.

"I'm not sure if we've learned anything useful, Herbie," says Violet, thrusting her hands into her pockets, "but . . . hey! What's this?"

Violet pulls something out of her pocket.

"Looks like a crumpled ball of paper," I say, a little underwhelmed.

"Wait, I *know* this ball of paper," Violet says, uncrumpling it. "It's the prescription card the mermonkey typed out for Eels. The one I threw away, which Erwin was playing with. Where is that pesky cat?"

But as we look around, we see that—just as he so often does—Erwin has vanished into thin air.

"Why would I want to keep this?" Violet says, waving the mermonkey card under my nose. "Unless . . . ?"

"Unless he's trying to tell us something?" I suggest. "About why Eels got *A Christmas Carol* and not some other book?"

"Or something," says Violet, snapping her fingers in sudden inspiration, "about why he *didn't*!"

"Eh?" I reply, scratching my head under my cap. But Violet is already running down Gazbaleen Alley toward Dolphin Square and the Eerie Book Dispensary.

CHAPTER 18

PANDORA LOST

It's late when we arrive at the bookshop, and Violet lets us in with her key. The fire in the great black marble fireplace is low in the grate, throwing a warm but distant glow on the books where they sleep on their shelves. The mermonkey, still and strange, sits in shadows, waiting.

"Violet, there you are," says Jenny, who is sitting with a book in one of the big armchairs. "I was worried. Hey, what's the hurry?"

Vi, who has already run into the next room, dodges back to wave a greeting at her guardian.

"Hi, Jenny!" she says. "Have you restocked any of the shelves upstairs yet? Or has anyone been dispensed a book from the same shelf as Sebastian Eels?"

"Apart from tidying up the mess Sebastian made in the corner," replies Jenny, pointing to the place where our enemy had cowered earlier, "I haven't touched a thing. Why . . . ?"

But Violet is already running deeper into the shop, heading for the stairs.

I do a side-on shrug and a "you know Violet!" grin for Jenny, and then hurry after my friend, who is leaping up the stairs three steps at a time. She has the mermonkey card in her hand—the one typed with the code:

$$2 - 1 - N - Cr - 66$$

"Vi, wait!" I call. "What are you expecting to find?"

"The truth," Violet calls back. "The truth about Sebastian Eels."

Upstairs, Violet heads into the first room, turns to the north wall, and looks up to the crimson shelf.

"Meow," says a voice, as I come skidding to a halt beside her. And even though one meow sounds much like another to me, this meow has a definite "I've been expecting you" twang to it.

Erwin is up on top of the bamboo ladder, which is hooked to the rail in the ceiling exactly where it was left earlier. The cat is somehow managing to balance on his bottom on a single rung, while he peers down at us with ice-blue, half-moon eyes.

"All right, puss," Violet says, "no need to look quite so smug."

She shoves the crumpled prescription card at me and rattles up the ladder to reach the crimson shelf.

"What's the last number?" Violet calls down, when she reaches the spot. "Sixty-six?"

"You know it is," I call back up.

Violet begins counting, from left to right, till she reaches the sixty-sixth book on the shelf.

"There's no gap," she calls down again. "Herbie, there's no gap!"

"I see," I say, even though I'm not sure I quite do. "Er, is that a good thing? Or is it the other thing?"

"Herbie!" Vi looks down at me. "If there's no gap, and Jenny hasn't refilled any shelves up here, then Eels can't have taken a book, can he?"

"Except he did," I point out. "*A Christmas Carol* by Charles Dickens. We all saw it flying through the air. It was hard to miss."

"Did we though?" Violet replies. "Or did we see what we were *meant* to see?"

"You're losing me, Vi," I admit.

"Look, the books are really tightly packed together," Violet says, tugging gently at a few spines with her finger. None of them move. "I don't think any book has been taken off this shelf today."

"Then, how . . ."

"Herbie, I think Eels brought *A Christmas Carol* with him," Violet says. "Up his sleeve, maybe, or . . . or tucked in his coat somehow. Maybe he picked it up from the pile he knocked over downstairs. He spent long enough in the corner groveling in the spilled books. I think he saw the Dickens and saw his *chance*. Herbie, he tricked us!"

"But that means . . ." I begin.

"Exactly!" Violet cries, "that means the book he was really prescribed is still here on the shelf. And when I count sixty-six spines along, I get to . . . this one. *This* is the book the mermonkey chose for Sebastian Eels!"

And Violet taps triumphantly on a slim blue book that I can just make out from down here.

"Fancy telling me what it is, Vi?" I say. "It's just that it's not much of a moment of triumph if we don't know what the book is called."

"There's no title on the spine," says Violet as she carefully works the book loose. It comes out slowly, with a little cloud of dust. She loops her arm through the ladder and uses both hands to open up to the title page. "It's called . . ."

Then she goes quiet.

"Vi?"

Violet starts to swing out from the ladder, as if suddenly paralyzed and only held on by her arm. She is staring so hard at the book, she seems to have forgotten to balance, and I'm suddenly certain she's going to fall off.

"*Vi!*" I yell, grabbing the ladder.

"Violet?" calls another voice, as Jenny—summoned by all the shouting up and down ladders—comes up the stairs. "Herbie, what's happening?"

"Come quickly!" I shout. "Violet's been bitten by a book!"

But Violet has already recovered from whatever shock she's had and is climbing down the ladder, clutching the book fiercely in one hand.

"Violet, what is it?" Jenny asks, entering the room. "What's wrong?"

Violet hands the book to her guardian and falls into a nearby chair, her hair crazier than ever. Jenny opens the book, and we read the title page together.

PANDORA LOST

or

The Tragedy of Mr. Ludo

But it's only when I read the name of the author that I understand why Violet has been stung into silence.

by

Peter Parma

And Peter Parma, in case you are new to town and don't know the whole sad story, is Violet's long-lost father.

CHAPTER 19

PETER PARMA

···

But I didn't know my dad had published any books," says Vi a short while later, when we are all back downstairs and Jenny has poked life back into the fire. Erwin is working hard to make a nest on Violet's lap, but not forgetting to also head-bump her chin from time to time in an encouraging way.

"I wasn't sure he'd even *written* any," Vi continues, "apart from his unpublished book about the malamander, that is. Jenny, why didn't you tell me?"

"I'm so sorry, Violet," Jenny replies, perching on the arm of the other armchair and looking embarrassed. "I just . . . forgot. Your dad was a young man when he vanished, only starting out on his writing career. But yes, he did have one book published already. And you're holding a copy of it in your hand."

"*Pandora Lost*," Violet repeats the title, turning the book over and over in her hand. There are embossed cogs on the front cover, and the title is stamped in brassy lettering. "What's it about?"

"Well," says Jenny, "funnily enough it's about the legend of Festergrimm. Interesting that it should surface just as Sebastian Eels returns to reopen the waxworks gallery."

"So, my dad knew all about Festergrimm's, too?"

"He researched the legend, yes," Jenny replies. "It's the story that first brought him to Eerie-on-Sea, years before you were born. It's probably how he first met Sebastian Eels, too. He wanted to find the truth—to dig behind the terrible clockwork robot and the mad inventor of the more popular versions of tale. But the book was not a success. First books often aren't."

"Did Eels write about Festergrimm, too?" I ask, remembering how Vi's dad clashed with Eerie's most famous writer so disastrously over the legend of the malamander.

"I don't think so," Jenny says. "But Sebastian wasn't happy to have another folklorist looking into *any* of the legends of Eerie-on-Sea, that's for sure. It was a sign of their rivalry to come. I really am sorry, Violet, not to have remembered about this book. It just got lost in the back of my mind all these years, and there weren't many copies printed. It's beautifully written though. How did you know it was there?"

"You've read it?" Violet asks, sidestepping Jenny's question with one of her own.

"Oh, yes," Jenny replies. "A long time ago. It's a sad tale, but your father's research brought to life a very moving and heartfelt version of the story, which certainly has the ring of truth. But you can find that out for yourself. Obviously, you must keep that copy, and I hope it's a comfort to read it."

Violet holds the book in both hands, tracing the cog design with her thumb. Then she opens the book and—as if Jenny and I are no longer there—she starts to read.

"What's a Pandora?" I whisper, leaning toward Jenny so as not to disturb Violet. "And how was it lost?"

"Not *what*, Herbie," Jenny replies, also whispering. "*Who*. Pandora was the name of Ludovic Festergrimm's daughter. The one who went missing and started it all."

"How, though?" I ask. "How did she get lost? I don't think I'm going to get a look in that book till Vi's finished. But as Lost-and-Founder, I need to know!"

"Well," Jenny begins. "It was two hundred years ago, back when Eerie-on-Sea was famous for its annual Winter Fair. People would come from miles around to buy and sell things here, though I think no one came from quite so far away as Ludo Festergrimm."

"It's funny to think," Violet says, lowering the book, "that Eerie-on-Sea once had such a fair and that people traveled here from far and wide. It seems like such a hard place to get to these days."

"That's because we've become used to roads and rails and airports," says Jenny. "We think of the sea as a barrier—a shark-filled trench to keep out the rest of the world. But in years gone by, when a road was little more than a mud track haunted by highwaymen—and no one could even imagine such a thing as an airplane—the sea was the fastest way to travel. The ocean is the gateway to the world, and back then the whole world came to us, every December, when the narrow streets of Eerie-on-Sea were lit with silk lamps and the glow of festive stalls. But of all the attractions of the Eerie Winter Fair, none was quite as magical as the tent of Ludovic Festergrimm, toy maker, clockwork master, and worker of wonders—known to all, with great affection, as Mr. Ludo."

Then Jenny makes a "may I?" gesture to Violet, who hands her the book. Jenny turns to the beginning and reads aloud.

"Mr. Ludo, Mr. Ludo!" the children would cry as the great man set up his stall in Fargazi Round, in the heart of town. "Where are you from, Mr. Ludo?"

"Ah, does it really matter," Mr. Ludo would invariably

reply, with a wink and a twinkle, "as long as I remember to bring . . . these?"

And he would release a handful of little painted cardboard butterflies to flutter above the jumping children—butterflies powered by nothing more than a tiny spring and even tinier gears. The mechanical marvels of Mr. Ludo's toy shop were expensive to buy, and far beyond the means of most in a small seaside town, but he always had a painted moth or butterfly for every child to catch for free.

As for the mechanical marvels themselves, well, it's said that you had to see them to believe them, and even then you might be tempted to think you'd fallen into a dream and imagined it all: steel birds that actually flew and sang with voices of silver; a life-size clockwork tiger made of bronze that prowled around, growling like the real thing; brass fish that swam about in a giant glass jar full of seawater, wherein a clockwork mermaid could be seen brushing her copper hair and waving at the crowd. Windup pinecone hedgehogs chased one another through a painted dollhouse, making tiny costumed dolls lift the hems of their skirts in fright. A horde of clockwork crabs and lobsters crept about the stall, snipping their scissor pincers, tapping at the fish as they swam by, and occasionally catching a hedgehog.

"How does this mousie work?" asked a girl, pointing to

a silver mouse that ran around a wooden maze. "How does he find his way?"

"A little invention of my own," explained Mr. Ludo, catching the mouse and presenting it the crowd. "Inside his head is a windup brain."

"No way!" said a watching fisherman, spraying his drink in disbelief. Several others made similar sounds of skepticism.

Mr. Ludo flipped open a panel on the mouse's silver head and showed something nestled in the gleaming workings within.

"Behold!" he said, beaming with pride as he pulled out a small lozenge of glass. Inside the crystal, tiny, tiny metal parts were spinning. "My gyroscopic regulator! It records where Mousie has been, and—and this is the important part—it stops him from going anywhere twice. That's all you really need to solve a maze."

"A bold claim," said a tall man dressed elegantly in black at the edge of the crowd. "And a valuable device, if what you say is true."

Mr. Ludo grinned and touched his hat.

"It is true, Your Lordship. Give him enough time, and little Mousie here can find his way through any labyrinth."

The toy maker replaced the crystal and popped the silver

mouse back in the wooden maze, whereupon the children moved the walls and tried to confuse him—without success but with many squeals of laughter.

And in among all these wondrous creations—shepherding them, presenting them to the crowd with precise gestures and a porcelain smile—was the undoubted star of the show: Mr. Ludo's mechanical daughter, Pandora.

Of course, everyone agreed that Pandora Festergrimm wasn't actually made of clockwork. That was impossible. True, her hair was as fine as spun gold, and her pretty face had a doll-like quality, but surely no mechanism in the world could move so fluidly, and no arrangement of even the finest silver bells could possibly create such a delightful voice. The girl, of course, was as human as you or I. She simply had to be.

People forgave Mr. Ludo this one obvious deception because of the spectacle of it all, and because of the clockwork butterflies for free, and because of the faces of the children when they found a windup pinecone hedgehog in the bottom of their Christmas stocking. But Pandora, even if she was wearing makeup and a costume and acting a part, was still uncanny. Lovely though she was, most folks agreed there was something a little eerie about Pandora Festergrimm. And maybe that's why they behaved as they did when she went missing.

CHAPTER 20

EERIE WINTER FAIR

It was the last day of the Winter Fair, and Eerie had received a fresh fall of snow. The people gathered around the warmth of street fires, enjoying the remaining hours of spiced fish cakes and mulled wine, as Mr. Ludo prepared for his famous final-night presentation. This was the moment when everyone who had purchased a clockwork marvel during the week would be presented with it as part of a musical light show. No one wanted to miss the spectacle. There were even fireworks at the end.

"Mr. Ludo! Mr. Ludo!" cried a voice.

A small boy ran up to the stall.

"What is it, child?" asked the head of Mr. Ludo, which

popped out from behind his embroidered curtain. "I am a little busy."

"I lost my flutterby down a drain!" the boy declared, as if reporting the most calamitous news that could befall anyone. "It's fallen down into the dark and gone!"

"Ah, no matter," Mr. Ludo replied, chuckling as he patted down the pockets of his motley coat. "I will no doubt find you another 'flutterby,' though it ought to be butter and fly, I think . . ."

"But I don't want another!" cried the boy, kicking up snow. "I loved my one. That's why Pandora's gone down to get it for me."

"What . . . ?" gasped Mr. Ludo, the color draining from his face. "What did you say?"

"Pandora," replied the boy. "But she can't find it. And now she can't get out. My flutterby is lost!"

Mr. Ludo cried out a foreign word that no one there knew, but which, by its force and sound, everyone seemed to understand. He seized the boy by the shoulders.

"Where is she?" he demanded. "Show me! Show me where Pandora went."

The boy pointed down a nearby side alley and promptly burst into tears.

Dropping the boy, Mr. Ludo tore through the snow

toward the alley, a small group of concerned people following after, passing the word to others that something had happened to the clockwork maker's daughter.

At the end of the alley, gaping dark in the new-fallen snow, was a large circular drain. There were bars of iron across the opening. One of them was broken and bent back at an extreme angle.

"What could have done that?" came a fearful voice from the onlookers.

"Pandora!" Mr. Ludo shouted down into the hole. "PANDORA!"

"Papa?" came a singsong voice, floating up out of the dark. It sounded impossibly far away.

"Pandora!" Mr. Ludo cried. "Thank the heavens you're all right. Don't move—I will fetch a rope."

"Wait, Papa," said the answering voice from far below. "There is a tunnel. Maybe there is another way out. I will see . . ."

"Pandora, no!" Mr. Ludo called back. "Wait there! I can pull you up." Then, turning to the crowd, he yelled, "A rope! For cog's sake, won't someone bring me a rope!"

"It is strange," came the voice of little Pandora, floating up from the deep as a fisherman ran for rope. "It is so dark. Yet, I feel I know this place. I wonder what is there . . ."

"Pandora, no!" cried Mr. Ludo, almost throwing himself down the hole. "Come back!"

Silence was his only answer. Silence, followed by an echoing, whirring sound that grew and grew until something emerged from the hole, fluttered a few times, then fell silently into the snow, its spring run down.

"My flutterby!" cried the little boy, snatching it up. "I'll keep you safe forever," he added, winding the toy's tiny spring, "and never lose you again." And with that he ran off to find his parents, not once looking back at the toy maker—who clutched uselessly at his motley coat, sank down into the snow, and turned a face of sudden despair to the hole. He shouted down into the engulfing dark like his whole life depended on it.

"PANDORA! PAN-DOR-AAA!"

But this time the silence was complete.

Pandora Festergrimm was gone.

"But what happened?" I ask, as Jenny reaches a pause in the story. "What did Mr. Ludo *do*?"

"He did what any loving parent would do," Jenny replies, with a glance at Violet. "He went down into the abyss to try to find his daughter."

"But he couldn't," says Violet. "Could he? Otherwise there wouldn't be a story, and we wouldn't be talking about any of this now."

"At first, people rallied around the desperate toy maker," Jenny explains. "A group of fisherfolk joined him on his expedition down into the passages beneath Eerie-on-Sea. These passages go on for miles and are a deadly labyrinth . . ."

"The Netherways," I say.

"The Netherways," she agrees. "Quite so. These days they are hard to access, but back then . . . Well, as I said, there was a drainage hole in the street. Mr. Ludo went down first, lowered by the fisherfolk, who then followed, one by one. Armed with lanterns, and each tied to one another by ropes around the waist, the band of men began exploring, calling Pandora by name. They were down there all night, but the girl was nowhere to be found."

" 'The following day,' " Violet says, gently taking her book back and continuing the reading from where Jenny left off, " 'a smaller band descended with Mr. Ludo, to search a different part of the Netherways. Then, when they, too, returned empty-handed, yet another group went down, smaller still. After three days, the fisherfolk took off their caps and paid Mr. Ludo their deepest condolences.'"

"We cannot give up!" cried the toy maker. "She's still down there, all alone!"

The fisherfolk shook their heads, but out of sympathy—and in honor of the great pleasure Mr. Ludo's toys and wonders always brought the town—they left him their ropes and lanterns.

The toy maker resumed the search alone, trying to map the passages he found, to make sense of the baffling maze as he searched for his daughter. The Winter Fair had long since ended, and the toy maker's tent was the only one left, neglected and covered in snow on Fargazi Round. Mr. Ludo, his hair wild and his eyes staring, would emerge for a few hours, blinking into the light to eat and drink, before resuming his lonely search.

"The Netherways will drive you mad," said the kindly townswoman who brought Mr. Ludo his meals. "Please stop, or you'll get lost down there, too."

But Mr. Ludo wouldn't stop. He remained in Eerie-on-Sea as the days became weeks and the weeks became years. He had a workshop built in the center of Fargazi Round and opened a toy shop there—offering his wondrous creations for sale, to raise funds to continue his search. But the magic of Mr. Ludo's wonders seemed to have gone out of them, just as the light had gone out of his eyes.

"I'm surprised he doesn't send an army of windup pinecone hedgehogs down there," muttered someone to his companion, as they passed by the workshop one day. "Let them find Pandora."

"What's the point?" said the companion. "No living human could find their way through the Netherways. The girl must be long dead by now."

Behind the shutters, working listlessly at some device or other, Mr. Ludo laid down his tools.

"No living human . . ." he muttered to himself. Then he cried, "Of course!"

Over the following months, little was seen or heard of the toy maker, apart from the endless banging and clanging of some great construction work that he was engaged in behind closed doors. Rumors began to spread that Mr. Ludo, deranged by grief, was breaking apart his clockwork toys and using the pieces to build something else. It would be something extraordinary, of course, but it must also be something massive. Larger than anything the toy maker had ever created in the past.

"And it's made of metal!" hissed a small child, his eye pressed to the shutters of Festergrimm's workshop. "With arms like tree trunks and lamps for eyes!"

"Come off it!" said another, disbelieving. "Let me see!"

"I liked Mr. Ludo more," said the youngest child there, "when he made flutterbys."

Soon after that, everyone in Eerie got to see what Ludovic Festergrimm had been working on.

CHAPTER 21

FESTERGRIMM'S GIANT

·······································

Violet turns the page and continues the strange tale of
the clockwork maker and his missing daughter.

*It was about this time that the people of Eerie-on-Sea
became alarmed enough to confront the crazed inventor in
his workshop. They gathered outside.*

*"Festergrimm!" called a leading fisherman, who spoke
for many. Beside him stood the mayor. "Festergrimm, come
out and explain yourself."*

*Few expected a reply, but—with a doom-laden creak—
the clockwork maker opened one of the doors to his workshop
and emerged, looking wilder than ever.*

"Explain myself?" he said. "What father should have to explain that he would do anything to find his lost child?"

"Aye, but what have you done?" said the fisherman. "The whole town is shaking with your hammering and clanging. What are you building?"

"I am building," replied the toy maker, "this!"

And he swung the doors fully open, revealing the gloom beyond. The townsfolk pressed forward to see what was inside.

"It's . . . it's a metal man!" said the fisherman.

"A metal giant!" said the mayor.

"Told you!" said a child to his friends.

"But . . ." the fisherman continued, waving everyone silent, "but what is it for?"

"It is for Pandora," said Mr. Ludo. "To find her in the Netherways and bring her safely home. Nothing can stand in its way!"

"But she's been down there for years!" exclaimed the mayor, losing the last of his sympathy for the toy maker's tragedy. "Hell's teeth, man, the girl must be long dead by now . . ."

"And even if she isn't," the fisherman interrupts, in a kinder voice, "how can a mere toy, however big, find the poor child?"

"Toy?" Festergrimm spat the word. "This is no toy."

Snatching up a crank handle from a bench in his

workshop, the clockwork maker climbed a wooden stepladder in front of the giant robot. He opened a large hatch in its chest, revealing a dizzying complexity of workings inside, and inserted the handle. Ludovic Festergrimm gave the handle three firm cranks to wind the clockwork spring.

Ck-Ck-Ck-Clunk, Ck-Ck-Ck-Clunk, Ck-Ck-Ck-Clunk!

Then he slammed the hatch shut, jumped down the ladder, and stood back from his creation.

"Awake!" he called. "Awake, I command you!"

In the robot's bronze head, two lamp eyes lit up with a fizzing electrical light that no one there had ever seen before. The head turned one way and then another with a fearsome metallic creak.

Festergrimm raised his hands in triumph and called again:

"Whom do you seek! Name the one who is lost!"

The robot tipped his great head forward, his eyes shining down upon his creator. In his grille of a mouth, an arrangement of iron bells began to swing.

PANG! *rang one of the bells.*

DONG! *rang another.*

RANG! *chimed a third.*

"The name!" cried the mad toy maker. "Tell me the name!"

"PANG, DONG, RANG," said the giant metal man again, with more certainty now, "PAN' DO' RA'!"

And with a mighty crash of great bronze feet, Festergrimm's robot stepped forward, emerging into the winter light and sending the people of Eerie-on-Sea staggering back in fear and confusion.

"It's alive!" cried a voice.

"How can clockwork do this?" cried another.

"All my art, all my science, every trick I know has gone into this!" Festergrimm replied. "And in its head, a tiny silver mouse that can solve any labyrinth—my gyroscopic regulator!"

But hardly anyone was listening to the toy maker now. Instead, the people ran in terror as the robot swung toward the short alleyway with the drainage hole, his limbs telescoping out until he was as tall as the buildings around him. One bronze shoulder caught on a nearby roof, and several tiles fell to shatter on the cobblestones.

"Call it off!" cried the mayor. "It will destroy our homes!"

But Ludovic Festergrimm—the man once loved as Mr. Ludo—would not call it off. Instead, he ran ahead of his robot, beckoning it impatiently, pointing at the gaping hole in the ground.

"Pandora!" he cried. "Find my little girl! Find Pandora!"

"PAN' DO' RA'," the metal man chimed in reply. He reached down a huge bronze fist, grasped the iron grate of the drain cover, and pulled it out of the pavement like a gardener pulls up weeds. Snow, ice, and cobblestones rained down around it.

Then the metal man lowered himself into the dark.

"PAN' DO' RA'!" rang the mouth bells once more, echoing up from the hole as Festergrimm's robot descended into the Netherways.

"Find her!" called the toy maker after his creation. "Find her, and bring her safely home!"

Violet stops reading and looks up at her audience.

"Are you all right, Herbie?"

And, well, that's the funny thing, isn't it?

Am I all right?

Because, despite the fact that I'm sitting in one of my favorite places, with my best friend and Jenny and Erwin the cat, beside a roaring fire, listening to a bonkers story about a mad inventor and his amazing robot . . . despite *all this*, something surprising is happening. And what is that something?

Well, see for yourself.

On each of my cheeks?

Tears!

"Herbie, are you *crying*?" Jenny leans forward, putting her hand on my shoulder. "I would have thought this tale of clockwork and inventions would be right up your street."

"It is!" I say, wiping my face quickly. "This street is Herbie Avenue, and I'd move in tomorrow if I could. But . . . there's something else about this story . . . almost like it's . . ."

"Yes?" says Violet. "Like it's what?"

"Like it's personal," I reply with a sigh. "Like I've heard it before. Except, I know I haven't. I mean, not in all this detail. I haven't read your dad's book, Vi, or anything like that. But I do know it somehow. I *know* about Pandora. I know how she felt to be lost. And somehow, deep down, lurking at the bottom of my mind like a . . . a . . . a bit of biscuit that fell off when I was dunking it in tea, I *know* where Pandora is."

"Herbie," Jenny says, with a smile, "you are a sensitive soul. And this is a sad story. But all these things happened two centuries ago, if they happened at all. What you are feeling is empathy—a sense of sympathetic connection with a character in a story. It's an emotional connection that does you credit, but that's all it is. I think we should stop reading now, if it's upsetting you. And it's so late! We should all go and get some sleep."

And so I shrug. Then I do one of my grins—the one I keep for when I want to make people think everything is all right.

Jenny suggests I stay the night, and Violet's keen on the idea, too, but I say no. I need to be seen at my cubbyhole tomorrow, bright and early, so I'd better get home. I wrap my coat around me, straighten my Lost-and-Founder's cap, and set off into the freezing night toward the hotel.

I don't think I'll sleep much. My mind is buzzing with everything that's happened, but something else is buzzing, too. I would say it's my heart, but that sounds soppy. It's something like that, though. Something deep inside me that has been set twanging by this legend of a lost girl, though I can't see why.

I kick a stone as I head round Tenby Twist, and it bangs off a shutter. But I'm too annoyed with myself to worry about the noise. Jenny's right—how can I have such a feeling of sadness for a character in a story who probably never existed anyway? It's stupid.

But as I slip behind the hotel bins and open my cellar window, my eyes are stinging once more, and another tear falls on the icy cobblestones.

EXQUISITELY CRAFTED

When I wake the next morning, it's a shame because I'm having a dream about freshly baked ginger cookies. I can almost smell them! I roll over and bury my face in my pillow so I can slip back into the sugary warmth of dreamland and . . .

"It's not a dream, Herbie," says a voice, and I feel my shoulder being shaken. "Wake up!"

"Hmmgnm?" I reply. Since when do cookies talk?

I open a reluctant eye.

Violet is there, in my Lost-and-Foundery, with four actual cookies gently steaming in a paper bag. She waves them under my nose.

"I was passing Mrs. Fossil's place," she explains. "She's been baking, so I thought I'd bring breakfast."

"What time is it?" I ask, sitting up.

"Late," Violet replies. "I think we both overslept. And after what happened last night, I was a bit worried. About you, I mean."

I take a cookie—so much better than my usual stale leftovers breakfast—and bite off a big bit. The strange feeling of sadness I felt last night almost seems like a dream itself. I don't really want to talk about it again.

"Thanks," I manage between chews. "But I'm fine. Did you read any more? Of the book, I mean. Did you find out what happened at the end?"

"Of course not!" Violet cries, kicking off her boots and jumping onto the bed in a shower of crumbs. "I didn't want to get ahead of you. We should read it together."

I look at Vi. When has she ever tried *not* to get ahead of me?

"Besides," she adds, pulling the copy of *Pandora Lost* from her coat pocket and opening it to where we left off. "There's loads more details in my dad's version of the legend than the doc's."

"I don't have time to read now, Vi," I reply, removing myself from the bed and heading around the corner to change. "I need to get busy, before Mr. Mollusc spots that I'm not."

"*Are* you all right, though?" Violet asks me a few minutes later, when I emerge again, fully dressed and with my cap more or less straight. Violet is now reaching the end of her second cookie. "I know you weren't exactly looking for this adventure."

"It's fine," I reply. "Honestly. I've just had enough of Sebastian Eels—forever up to no good and always knowing more about everything than anyone else. Even about me!"

I say this last bit because it's true. I'm the boy who washed up on the beach in Eerie-on-Sea in a crate of lemons years ago, with no memory of his past and no idea where he came from. And yet Sebastian Eels has always hinted that maybe he does know.

"So, you're OK to investigate further?" Violet asks. "Despite the severed finger, the creepy waxworks, and the crazy, trident-wielding author?"

I nod.

"Great! And no more Nope-vember?"

"Nope," I reply. "I mean, yup. I mean, *yope!*"

I take the last cookie.

"I *mean*," I explain, "it's time we did something about Sebastian Eels, once and for all. And I think I know how to start."

⚙

It's a little while later, and I've left the sign on my cubbyhole flipped to CLOSED. Mr. Mollusc made a beeline for me when he saw this, to demand an explanation, but I just said, "Time and tide wait for no man when there's lost-and-foundering to be done," and walked away.

Now, Vi and I find ourselves outside the huge wooden doors of the Eerie Museum, ringing the bell pull for Dr. Thalassi.

"Why are we here?" asks Violet. "Surely this is the last place we'll find Sebastian Eels?"

"I'm sure it is," I agree. "But this is where we'll find the thing he's been pestering me to return. At least, if I'm right about what it is."

"Really?" Violet says, but the doc opens the door before I can answer.

"Violet? Herbie?" says Dr. Thalassi. "Is something the matter?"

Eerie-on-Sea's medical man and curator of the Eerie Museum has his sleeves rolled up and his glasses low on his Roman nose. It looks like he was settling down to a long day of counting, curating, and fussing over his displays and wasn't prepared for visitors.

"Nothing's the matter, Doc," I reply. "I'm just here for Clermit. Remember? My clockwork hermit crab you were help-ing me fix?"

"Ah, indeed," says the doc, pushing his specs back up onto his brow and gesturing us in. "It's good that you've come. As I said yesterday, I'm afraid it's not the best news."

We follow Dr. Thalassi into the museum—past the fabu-lous fish-shaped bottle that is displayed in pride of place at the entrance—and into the main gallery, full of glass cabinets of weird and wonderful things that the history of Eerie-on-Sea has left us. Above it all hangs suspended the vast skeleton of a whale.

"The fact is, I've had to admit defeat," the doc continues as he leads us through his study and into the workroom beyond. Judging by his face, he is not happy admitting anything of the sort.

"But I must ask, Herbie," he says as he lifts a large dust sheet off a workbench. "Where on earth did you get this toy of yours? It's fabulously complex."

Spread across the bench are the ruins of Clermit.

His pearly shell, which once contained his clockwork mechanism, is lying in three broken parts. The clockwork itself is splayed out methodically in the center of the desk, with the doc's vast array of precision tools lying all around.

"I've spent days on it," Dr. Thalassi explains. "It was pretty badly smashed, as you know. So? Do you want to tell me where it comes from?"

The truthful answer is that this clockwork device was once owned by Sebastian Eels, who used it against us, only for it to bravely switch sides when I made it a solemn promise. But I don't think I can say all that to the doc.

"It's a lost thing," I reply with a shrug. "It came to my Lost-and-Foundery, and I . . . I promised I'd return it one day to its rightful owner. It's my job, after all."

When I look up, I see that the museum curator is peering into my eyes from beneath one spectacularly arched eyebrow.

"I see," he says after an awkward silence. "It's just that this is no ordinary toy, Herbie. This clockwork is exquisitely crafted, beyond anything I've seen, and even contains a mysterious part I cannot begin to fathom. It's the work of a true master. And it's old—*really* old. Yet you say it was just handed in to lost property? Like an odd sock or a forgotten suitcase?"

I do a shrug. Then I do a grin. *Then*, because the doc still has his eyebrow dialed up to ten, I do another shrug, only bigger this time.

"Very well." Dr. Thalassi lets out a sigh. "Have it your way, Herbert Lemon. In any case, I'm sorry to say that I am unable to fix the device. I think I can see how the parts connect, but it's just so mind-bogglingly hard to assemble them. The shell can be glued, of course, but I believe the best thing would be to just display the whole exhibit as it is."

"Display it?" Violet says.

"Exhibit?" I cry.

"Well, yes." The doc looks a bit sheepish. "Even if someone came to reclaim it from you now, Herbie, it's too damaged to be much good to them. I hope I can persuade you to donate it to the museum."

"There must be something more you can do!" I reply.

"There isn't." The doc's eyes harden. "But as an artifact of great historical value, I feel I must insist that it belongs in my . . . in the museum."

"Wait, Doctor," Violet says. "Did you say there was a mysterious part in the clockwork? What did you mean?"

"I mean"—the doc takes up a pair of fine, rubberized tweezers—"this!"

And with great delicacy, Dr. Thalassi inserts the tweezers into the complexity of gears and cogs in poor Clermit's shattered body and extracts something that sparkles like ice in the lamplight.

It's a tiny crystal lozenge of cut glass, with the gleam of gold inside.

CHAPTER 23

MOST POWERFUL THING

The gyroscopic regulator!" I gasp.

"The what?" says Dr. Thalassi in surprise.

"Oh, um . . ." I am suddenly unsure whether a grin or a shrug is the best approach. "Just something I heard about recently. Er, what do *you* think it is, Doc?"

"Well, it's a crystal that contains a single gold wire," the doctor replies. "Take a look for yourselves." And he places it carefully on a little steel anvil on the workbench, with an angle-poised magnifying glass attached.

"I have no idea what it can be for," says Dr. Thalassi.

Violet and I lean in together. There is indeed a thin strand of bright golden thread, no thicker than a human hair, running right through the crystal lozenge. I glance at Vi and find she's glancing back at me.

The gyroscopic regulator, as described in Peter Parma's book, was a crystal like this, yes, but one that contained tiny gears and many moving parts. And it was in a silver mouse, not a windup crab.

Violet twitches her nose at me, in a way that seems to say, *So, NOT the gyroscopic regulator, then?*

I waggle my ear back, and I hope she understands: *No, this can't be the regulator.*

But in that case, what is it?

"At one end of the crystal is a small brass disk," I observe, peering even closer. "Like one half of a snap. Do you think it plugs in somewhere, Doc?"

"Plugs in?" Dr. Thalassi looks confused. "That would suggest something electrical. But this clockwork device is purely mechanical, Herbie. Why would a crystal plug in?"

Well, if I knew things like that, I wouldn't be asking for help to fix Clermit, now, would I? But I don't say that. Instead, I take the tweezers and pick up the little crystal lozenge. After a bit more peering around, I locate, deep in the heart of Clermit's dazzling mechanism, a tiny brass cup—like the *other* half of a snap—and, with great care, I plug the crystal into it.

ting

Nothing happens.

Then, before three pairs of astonished eyes, something *extraordinary* does.

Clermit, spread out as he is like a dissected creature in a biologist's lab, suddenly pulls himself together. All his parts, all his limbs—every little cog and gear of him—gather together and reassemble, as the tiny bells in his music box ring out a bright snatch of melody. It's as if the work the doc was only able to half finish has just finished itself by . . . well, by *magic*.

Or something very like it.

"Great heavens above!" gasps Dr. Thalassi, his spectacles falling onto his nose as he slumps back into a chair. "That . . . shouldn't happen."

"I think," I say, returning the tweezers carefully to their place, "that I'd like you to glue the shell back together, Doc. With the mechanism inside, of course. I'll take Clermit now, if you please, with thanks for all you've done."

Dr. Thalassi jumps up. "But, Herbie . . ." he says, laying his hand possessively over the clockwork. "I can't just let you take such a . . . a . . . *wonder* as this. Especially after what I've just seen . . ."

"Have you ever heard of the deepest secret of Eerie-on-Sea?" I ask the doc then, right out of the blue.

Dr. Thalassi stares at me.

"Why would you ask such a question?"

"Well?" Violet insists. "Have you?"

The doc sits back in the chair again. Then he sighs and starts cleaning his glasses nervously.

"You know, when my parents first came to this country," he says eventually, "they insisted I went into a good profession. So, when I grew up, I became a London doctor and a man of science. I've always put my trust in what I can understand and measure, Herbie, you know that."

I give an encouraging half smile and wonder where this is going.

"But *something* drew me to Eerie-on-Sea, though I'd barely heard of the place. And *something*—whatever that something may be—drew me to become the curator of this museum on the edge of the world, with its strange collection, and"—he nods at Clermit—"to witness eerie things. So now, after everything, this man of science is forced to admit that some things can't be understood or measured, and that Eerie-on-Sea even has a way of getting into your *dreams* . . ."

"Your dreams?" Violet repeats, but Dr. Thalassi just shakes his head and puts his glasses back on.

"In the end," he continues, "despite all my learning, all I really know is this: If there is such a thing as a deepest secret of Eerie-on-Sea, I suspect you two already know more about it than I ever will."

Violet and I look at each other. We don't know what to say.

"So, if you tell me you must take this treasure back, Herbie," the doc concludes, lifting his hands in surrender, "who am I to refuse? You are Lost-and-Founder here, not me."

"Thanks!" is all I can blurt out.

"But," he adds, "I need you to promise me you will take good care of it. And yourselves. And not do anything foolish. Understand?"

The eyebrow is back up again.

"I swear on my cap, Doc," I reply, "that we won't do anything that doesn't need to be done. And that's a Herbie promise."

"Very well." The doc nods. "And now maybe you two should wait in my office while I work on the broken shell. The glue is a special kind, museum-grade, and stinks like a skunk's pajamas. I'll call you when it's ready."

⚙🔘✿

Back in Dr. Thalassi's office, I pull the door of the workroom closed so Vi and I can talk in private.

"Do you think," Violet asks, "that the doc recognizes Clermit as Mr. Ludo's work? Because surely he must be!"

"Of course he does," I reply. "The doc's not stupid."

"And do you also think," she adds, "that Clermit is really the thing that Eels is trying to get back from you?"

"I can't imagine what else it could be," I say. "And it was

Eels who used Clermit against us in the first place, back in our Gargantis adventure. I reckon Sebastian Eels is after any clock-work left over from Mr. Ludo's time. But he's *not* getting his hands on Clermit."

Soon enough, Dr. Thalassi emerges from his workroom, holding the pearlescent shell in his hands.

"There," he says, "good as new. Well, not really *new*. But you will never find the join—I have a very steady hand."

Then, with obvious hesitation—as if hoping that even now I'll change my mind and donate my little clockwork helper to the museum—he hands Clermit back to me.

"Thanks, Doc," I say, tugging the shell from the curator's reluctant fingers. "Oh," I add, as we get ready to leave, "I have a question. About the legend of Festergrimm and his robot."

"Yes?" says the doc.

"Would clockwork be enough to power a giant bronze robot?" I ask. "In a story, that is. I mean, I know it's good for model mice or a windup cardboard flutterby . . . I mean, butterfly. But could it really drive something big and powerful? Could clockwork alone bring a robot to life?"

Dr. Thalassi chuckles.

"Herbie, in a story you can do anything. That's why we like stories, after all. And there are actually lots of legends about people creating artificial men and women and bringing them to life. You've heard of Frankenstein, haven't you?"

"Well, yes . . ." I begin, but the doc never gives one example when three will do, and he's already slipping into lecture mode.

"Back in the sixteenth century, a man called Rabbi Loew formed a creature called a Golem out of clay and brought it to life with holy power. And in ancient times, the Greek god Hephaestus built a giant metal statue, summoned to life by ichor, the blood of the gods. And then . . ."

"Did Mr. Ludo . . ." I say loudly, to interrupt. "I mean, did Ludovic Festergrimm have these things? Holy power or that icky stuff?"

"Not in the stories I've heard," says Dr. Thalassi. "But that doesn't mean there wasn't *something* extra that animated his clockwork robot and gave it purpose. Surely you've heard enough of the legend to guess what that might be."

Violet and I look at each other. Then we both shrug.

"He was a father," the doc explains, "who had lost someone dear to him, more dear than anything: his only child! In his desperation to get his daughter back, I'd say Ludo Festergrimm had something especially powerful to put into his clockwork robot— maybe the most powerful thing of all."

"But what?" says Vi. "What's the most powerful thing of all?"

Dr. Thalassi smiles, as if the answer is as clear as day.

"Love," he says.

CHAPTER 24

CAKES AND CURSES

It's not till we've left the museum that I slip Clermit back under my cap, where he belongs. At least, where he belongs until I can return him to his rightful owner. But what if his rightful owner is actually this long-dead clockwork maker of legend? What then?

"Aren't you going to wind up Clermit?" says Violet as we head back into the town.

"I forgot to bring his winder," I admit. "But I'm not sure about winding him up just yet, Vi. There are already a lot of moving parts in this mystery, without adding any more."

"Oh, Herbie!"

Violet isn't impressed. She sees Clermit as one of the team on our adventures: Vi, me, Clermit, and . . .

"Prrp?" says a feline voice, and Erwin slides down a nearby drainpipe. He entwines himself around Violet's ankles and rumbles with purr.

"Hey, puss." Violet scoops him up to carry as we go. "Anything to report?"

"We-ow!" he replies, with a significant look. And then, as we turn the corner into Fargazi Round, we see what he means and skid to a halt in amazement.

"Someone's been busy!" I exclaim at the sight of the old waxworks gallery.

The sign—the one that says FESTERGRIMM'S WAXWORKS— is already fixed back up over the doors. The painted robot head stares down at us from between glowing light-bulb letters. Two carpenters I recognize as fisherfolk from the harbor are on the roof, mending the broken window. Another fisherman has begun painting the outside of the building itself, and one of the waxworks—the dread pirate Purple Pimm, with her feathered hat and cutlass—is standing to one side of the open doorway, looking fearsome and waxy in the light of day. Several locals are hanging around, chatting in excitement, and I can't help feeling that none of this looks like Sebastian Eels is working on some dastardly secret plan.

"It looks," I say aloud, "as if Eels is doing exactly what he said he'd do: reopen the old place for visitors."

"Here," says a voice, and a girl emerges from the gallery and hands us a leaflet from a pile in her hands. I vaguely recognize her, too, as a daughter of one of the local fishing families.

"What's this?" Vi asks, turning the leaflet over.

"Reward," says the girl, and she nods to a cardboard box full of metal odds and ends beside the waxwork pirate. "Mr. Eels is offering it. For anyone who has any old bits of clockwork they don't want. Did you know the waxworks is opening again? It's gonna be amazing!"

"And did *you* know," Violet snaps, shoving the leaflet back in the girl's hands, "that *Mr. Eels* is a crook? How can you work for him?"

"Meh," the girl says. "All that stuff about him being dodgy, I reckon it's just rumors. I've never seen any of it, anyway. Besides, he pays well, and there's nothing much else to do this time of year, is there? *And* he says he'll make a waxwork of me. As a mermaid!"

Violet looks like she's about to explode, so I steer her away. We can hear banging and hammering sounds from down in the basement gallery beneath Festergrimm's. Mr. Eels, it seems, is very busy indeed.

"Hey, Herbie!" the girl calls after us. "I forgot, but the boss was asking for you. Says you have something that belongs to him. Wait, I'll go and tell Mr. Eels you're here . . . Oh, he must have heard that, he's just coming out."

"Must dash!" I call back urgently. "Bye!"

And Violet and I hurry away, with Erwin close behind. But before we can leave the square entirely, Violet grabs my arm.

"Let's see what happens next," she whispers, and pulls me behind the building, where we can spy on things.

Sebastian Eels walks out of the waxworks. He's wearing that gruesome apron again.

"Did I hear you say Herbert Lemon was here?" he demands of the girl with the leaflets.

"Yeah," she replies, "he was. With his silly cap and goofy face. But he pretended to be in a big hurry and ran away."

"Hmm," says Eels darkly. Then, from our place of concealment, we see him walk over to the cardboard box full of bits and start poking about in it.

"Junk," he says, as he lifts up various broken objects, only to drop them back in. "I said clockwork, not old toasters . . . wait a minute." He stoops and grabs something from the bottom of the box. From where we are hiding, it looks like a skeleton arm made of metal, with a flubbery hand attached.

"Who left this here?" he demands, waving the arm. "Quickly, now—who was it?"

"Her over there," says the girl, pointing at Mrs. Fossil's Flotsamporium opposite. "The beachcomber. She said she didn't need a reward. Hey, maybe I can have it instead . . . ?"

"Wendy Fossil," Sebastian Eels says, waving the girl's suggestion away. He strokes his chin with the waxwork hand. "Maybe it's time to turn up the heat under our dear neighbor."

He strides over to Mrs. Fossil's shop door and hammers on it with his fist. There's no answer, so he hammers again and again, until eventually the door opens, just a crack, and Mrs. Fossil peers out.

"Good morning, Wendy," Sebastian Eels croons. "Not open today?"

"Oh!" Mrs. Fossil gasps, as if she has just opened the door to her worst nightmare. "I . . . I don't feel too well today, so . . ."

She begins to close the door, but Sebastian Eels shoves the arm into it.

"Not so fast," he snaps. Then, glancing around as if remembering that he has an audience, he says, in a more pleasant tone, "I was just wondering, now that we are to be neighbors, if you would perhaps make a big pot of tea for my workers. And do you still bake? I'm sure we'd all love some of your delicious cake."

There's a general murmur of approval at this idea from the

fisherfolk working on the gallery, and the leaflet girl says, "Yes, please!"

"Oh!" Mrs. Fossil gasps again.

"Let me come in and make the order properly," Eels says, as if he's simply being helpful. He forces the door open and walks inside. "And we can have a little chat about where you found this lovely rotten arm . . ."

He closes the door behind him.

"Poor Mrs. Fossil!" I whisper.

"Bur-*wow*," agrees Erwin.

"Where *did* Mrs. F find that arm?" Violet whispers back. "I'd like to know that, too."

"We'll ask her later," I reply, "when the coast is clear."

"Or," says Violet, turning to me with a glint in her eye, "we can find out now by listening at the window . . ."

And before I can stop her, Violet has jogged over to the front of the Flotsamporium and slipped behind a barrel of twisty driftwood walking sticks. Loudest Girl has gone back into the gallery, and the fisherfolk on the roof show no sign of being interested in Violet and her cat, so I dash over to join them behind the barrel. Together we press our ears to the shop window and try to hear what we can.

"Don't take that tone with me!" Sebastian Eels is saying to

Mrs. Fossil, followed by something too muffled to understand.

Mrs. Fossil is mostly replying with "oh!" but we do manage to catch "that's the only bit I have left, I promise!" and "I never want anything to do with waxworks again!"

The next exchange is so mumbly that I give up with my ear and turn to look instead. Through the sea-spray grubbiness of the Flotsamporium window, between the jars of sea glass, I see Mrs. Fossil fussing over her biggest kettle, while Sebastian Eels looms nearby, looking threatening and nasty. Then he suddenly turns to leave. Violet and I barely have enough time to duck behind the barrel.

Eels yanks the shop door open, sending the bell dinging like crazy. Then he turns and says one last thing to the startled beachcomber.

"You'd better cooperate, Wendy Fossil. Or I'll remind everyone in our town of your grubby little family secret."

And with this, he slams the door and marches back into Festergrimm's.

CHAPTER 25

GRUBBY LITTLE SECRETS

As soon as Eels is gone, Violet slides out from behind the barrel and opens the door to the Flotsamporium with a *TING!*

"Oh!" Mrs. Fossil jumps with fright, nearly sending a tray of scones bouncing across the counter. "Violet! Herbie! It's you! I'm . . . I'm not really open today."

"And yet, here you are making tea," Violet points out, "tea and cakes for Sebastian Eels. You mustn't let him bully you like that. He can boil a kettle himself, can't he?"

Mrs. Fossil gives a desperate, snaggletooth grin and slides the scones onto the safety of a wooden board, beside a pot of jam.

"It's not really bullying," she explains, "not *really*. Not to give tea and scones to the hardworking fisherfolk. And the bystand-ers, maybe, if they want some. I . . . I don't mind. Honest!"

"Are you sure?" says Vi as we follow Mrs. F into the kitchen at the back of the shop. Though the Flotsamporium is closed, there is a warm smell of fresh baking and the familiar sense of a jumbled welcome among the beachcombed treasures. Sunlight rainbows across the floor through the sea glass in the window. "We heard what Eels said," Vi adds. "We *know* he's threatening you."

Mrs. Fossil goes pale.

"You *heard*?"

"We didn't hear everything," I explain, quickly. "But what were you doing with that waxwork arm, Mrs. F? And why did you give it to Eels?"

"It's not what you think!" Mrs. Fossil looks distraught. "I don't want anything to do with that place, I swear. But that arm has been in my attic for years, and this was a good chance to get rid of it. Now I don't have any connection with that horrid place at all, and that's how I want it to stay."

"But what is your connection?" Violet asks. "Why are you the caretaker of Festergrimm's Eerie Waxworks, when you're clearly terrified of the place. Why did *you* have the key all these years, Mrs. Fossil?"

"Because . . ." Mrs. Fossil replies, wringing her hands. Then she drops her voice to a worried whisper, "because it was my ancestor Felix Fossil who created the waxworks in the first place. Festergrimm's was our family business!"

⚙○✿

It's a little while later, and Mrs. Fossil has delivered tea and scones to the workers outside. When she comes back, she finds Violet and me sitting, waiting. We have Violet's dad's book out, ready to discover more of the legend of Mr. Ludo and his amazing robot. But we can't quite concentrate on that yet.

"Festergrimm's is your family business?" I blurt out. "I thought Lady Kraken owned it!"

"Well, she does," Mrs. F admits, rocking back and forth on her rubber boots in the middle of her shop. "She owns the building, just as she owns a lot of the town. But it was my great-great-grandpappy Felix who opened it up as a tourist attraction. I'd probably be running it today, if the . . . the *thing* that happened hadn't happened."

"Thing?" Vi and I say together. "What thing?"

"The scandal!" Mrs. Fossil stops rocking and covers her face with her hands. "Oh, it's taken years for everyone to forget. What if Sebastian brings it all up again? What if people remember what the Fossil family has done?"

Violet leads the distraught beachcomber over to a deck chair by the stove. I go into the kitchen and make some more tea.

There are some scones left, so I pile jam on one and balance it on Mrs. F's mug when I bring it through.

"You don't have to tell us, of course," says Violet, "but I can't believe you would be involved in an actual scandal, Mrs. F. Are you sure it's not just a misunderstanding?"

"If only it was!" Mrs. Fossil cries. "But I really don't want to bring it all up again. Thanks for the tea, my dears. And now, please let's talk about something else. What's that book you have there?" she adds, nodding at Violet's lap. "Why don't you tell me what exciting things you two are up to and take my mind off these horrid waxworks?"

"This book," Violet declares, holding it up for us both to see, "is the *real* book Sebastian Eels got from the mermonkey. And it was written by my dad! It's all about the legend of Ludo Festergrimm and his lost daughter Pandora, and . . ."

Mrs. Fossil, who had started to get some color back in her cheeks, drops her scone and shrinks back into her deck chair.

"Then Sebastian really does know!" she cries. "He will ruin me!"

"Maybe we should go," I say, but Violet waves me to sit.

"Mrs. Fossil," she says. "Wendy. We need to find out what happened all those years ago—why the legend of a giant metal man that hardly seems real is connected to a waxworks tourist attraction that definitely is. We don't want to make things tricky for you, but it sounds like you know a thing or two about it all. Maybe, if you can help us work out the truth about what Eels is up to, it might help you, too?"

Mrs. Fossil peers out from between her fingers.

"Where . . ." she asks, "where did you get to in the legend?"

"Well." Violet flicks the book open. "Mr. Ludo, the genius clockwork maker, had built a windup bronze robot to search for his missing daughter, who had got herself lost in the Netherways beneath Eerie-on-Sea. He had just set the robot going, and it had smashed its way down through a drain, but we don't know what happened next."

"There's no mystery about what happened next," Mrs. F says. "The robot disappeared. Soon people started to forget about it, like it was nothing more than a strange dream. Only mad-haired Mr. Ludo remained to remind them that anything eerie had happened at all. He could be seen, day after day, pacing around Fargazi Round, waiting for the robot to return. He seemed genuinely to believe it would find little Pandora and lead her home."

"But it didn't?" Vi suggests.

Mrs. Fossil shakes her head.

"It did come back though," she says. "Maybe see what the book says, Violet. I'm sure your dad knew more about it all than I do."

"'One night,'" Violet reads, holding the book in both hands, "'while Eerie slept, many weeks after the town last saw the fearsome robot disappear underground, there came a terrible crash from one of the houses. The bronze robot, still whirring with his clockwork engine, had climbed his way back up and was smashing from cellar to cellar, leaving terrible destruction in his wake.'"

"Makes sense," I say. "The gyroscopic regulator in the robot's head was driving it to search everywhere at least once. It probably saw the cellars as part of the Netherways."

"Probably . . ." said Violet. "Anyway, 'Mr. Ludo, after his long wait for news, ran to the robot—when it finally emerged on the street—to try and stop it.'"

"Where is she?" he cried. "Where is Pandora?"

"PAN' DO' RA'," chimed the bells in the metal man's mouth.

To deactivate the robot, Mr. Ludo climbed up its front and opened its chest plate. But before he could flip the switch, a group of fisherfolk—responding to the screams and sounds of destruction—ran to attack the machine with boat hooks and whaling spears.

"What are you doing?" cried the robot's creator in horror, as a boat hook smashed something out of the metal giant's workings. As this thing fell to the ground, the robot's eye lamps—which had glowed with a golden light till now— suddenly turned bloodred. He swung his fist at the fisherfolk, scattering them and demolishing the front of a nearby house.

"Stop!" Mr. Ludo cried, jumping down and scouring

the ground, trying desperately to find the fallen part. "You
don't need to fight it!"

But the fisherfolk, watching their homes being destroyed,
didn't agree. They were soon joined by a growing crowd
of townsfolk, who threw rocks and bottles—anything they
could find—to defend their town. And the robot, seemingly
out of control now, swung his immense bronze fists and
fought back.

"Don't damage his head!" Ludo Festergrimm begged
the crowd, as rocks bounced off the metal giant, dent-
ing it all over. "The regulator is fragile. It has mapped the
Netherways! I need it to find my daughter!"

"There!" I say, triumphantly interrupting Violet. "Told you."

"Well done, Herbie," Violet replies, before continuing the book.

No one was listening to Mr. Ludo now, in spite of his grief.
He had unleashed a clockwork monster, and the folk of
Eerie-on-Sea were determined to bring it down.

"Call out the army!" cried the mayor, sending a run-
ner to the castle. At this time the castle was still used as a
barracks, and a company of infantrymen was dispatched,
armed with muskets and sabers, to deal with the situation.

"Never mind the army," said Lord Kraken. "Signal the navy! There is a ship in the bay, and this is a job for heavy guns."

"Wait, what?" I blurt out, interrupting again because I can't help it. "Did you say *Lord* Kraken?"

"The head of the Kraken family back then," explains Mrs. Fossil, who had been listening intently, clutching her deck chair. "He was Lady Kraken's great-great-grandfather, or thereabouts. He was also an admiral, so it shouldn't be surprising he could signal for a ship. And maybe he was right, because that ship saved the town in the end. And changed my family's fortunes forever."

Turning the page, Violet reads on.

CHAPTER 26

LORD KRAKEN'S ASSISTANT

....

Soon the robot had left the town and was climbing
Eerie Rock, heading for the cliff tops, followed by
the braying mob. Ludo Festergrimm, who had been
injured in the fighting, was limping after them, pleading
that the robot's spring was winding down and that he would
stop soon.

But Eerie-on-Sea had had enough.

By now much of the town was in ruins, and fires raged
unchecked. People had been hurt, and many more had become
homeless. Those soldiers who could still fight were taking
shots at the monster as he climbed, and the fisherfolk were

forming a ring around it, carrying flaming torches, ropes, and improvised weapons, determined to finish it off.

And then, just as he reached the cliff's edge, the metal man creaked to a halt. His spring had finally run down.

"PAN' . . . PANG . . . DONG . . . ra' . . ."

The robot's bells fell silent, and he stood statue-still.

"My regulator!" gasped Ludo Festergrimm, pushing his way to the front of the mob. "Let me get my regulator."

He began to climb his clockwork giant, reaching for its head.

But he had forgotten one thing: Lord Kraken's ship.

In those days, war was never far away, and a heavily armed frigate patrolled Eerie Bay. In answer to the admiral's signal, it had sailed in close to the town, its commander searching the burning buildings with his telescope for signs of an enemy. Then he beheld the astonishing spectacle of a bronze giant, standing on the cliff top, gleaming in the firelight.

"That looks like it shouldn't be there," he said as he snapped his telescope shut. He ordered his men to take aim.

"Fire!"

Three cannons erupted.

And three cannonballs flew straight and true.

Up on the cliff top, the bronze giant was engulfed in an explosion of fire and light. Pieces of robot, and of the man who had built it, were flung high into the air, to rain down across the rooftops of Eerie-on-Sea and onto the beach far below. Ludovic Festergrimm and his mighty creation were destroyed in an instant.

Violet stops reading and looks up.

"So, Mr. Ludo really was blown to pieces," she says. "Horrible!"

"Very," I agree with a shudder. "But I don't see how any of this is connected to you, Mrs. F. It's a crazy tale of crowds and cannons, trigger-happy lords and clockwork gone wrong."

"You will soon, my dears," Mrs. Fossil replies. "Skip to the bit about Lord Kraken taking charge of the remains."

Violet flicks forward a page or two, and then starts reading again.

By the end of the following day, Eerie-on-Sea was counting the cost of the battle and had already begun repairs. Lord Kraken decreed that all parts of the fearsome metal giant should be recovered, lest they fall into the wrong hands. He offered a rich reward for even the smallest part, so that no scrap of clockwork should remain at large. He had everything brought to the mad toy maker's workshop, which—since it was built on Kraken land, anyway— he confiscated. Once everything that had been found was gathered inside, Lord Kraken shut the workshop doors and turned the key on this chapter of Eerie history forever.

"If only!" Mrs. Fossil shakes her head at this. "That may be the end of the Festergrimm legend as most people know it, Violet, but it doesn't mean there isn't more to tell."

The beachcomber glances nervously at the door of her shop, checking that no one is about to come in. Then she gets to her feet and unhooks something from behind the clutter on the wall. It's a framed picture, the corner of which we noticed earlier. Mrs. F holds it up, and we see an old-fashioned watercolor sketch of a whiskery man with a screwdriver behind his ear and a snaggletooth grin. Judging by the fancy frame, this picture was once an object of great pride. Now it is hidden beneath dust and cobwebs.

"Felix Fossil!" Vi and I say at the same time, because who else can it be. "Your great-great-grandfather!"

Mrs. F gives a nod and flicks away a few dead flies.

"Good old Felix," she says. "He lived in this very house, long before it was a Flotsamporium, though he died before I was born.

He was a blacksmith by trade—did all of Eerie's metalworking and a bit of dentistry on the side. But he was cleverer than that. Always dreamed bigger than horseshoes and boat repairs, did our Felix. And thanks to Lord Kraken, he got his chance."

"What do you mean?"

"A man like Lord Kraken doesn't offer rewards for parts of a smashed clock-

work machine for the fun of it, does he?" says Mrs. Fossil. "He wanted Mr. Ludo's secrets for himself. But he wouldn't get his own hands dirty. Oh, no! He needed help from someone who knew about machines, so he made Felix Fossil his assistant. And Felix, who was every bit in awe of the toy maker's wonderful clockwork as His Lordship, didn't need much persuading.

"So, a new legend was born. Folks say that Lord Kraken had a secret tunnel built from his grand house straight to the basement of Mr. Ludo's workshop. They say that for years, banging and clanging could be heard from deep beneath Fargazi Round, as Lord Kraken and his assistant worked deep underground, in a secret clockwork laboratory, to reassemble Festergrimm's terrible robot."

"You mean . . ." I gasp, "they *fixed* it? They rebuilt the bronze robot?"

"I wouldn't say that, Herbie," Mrs. Fossil replies. "Kraken did his best to find all the bits, but there were always pieces missing. Goodness only knows how many replacement parts Felix had to make from scratch. But one piece in particular—the most important part, the piece Lord Kraken desired most of all—was never found."

"The head," Violet says. "The head of Festergrimm's robot, with the gyroscopic regulator inside."

"That's right." Mrs. Fossil nods. "When the robot was blasted to bits, its head flew clear over the town. Some say it landed in the sea and became a home for crabs. Others that it got stuck on the spire of Saint Dismal's Church and was blasted away by lightning. For years afterward, people would come forward swearing to have found the head of Festergrimm's robot and trying to claim the king's reward that Lord Kraken offered, only to be sent away because they simply had an old bucket or a broken kettle. The actual head was never seen again."

"So, Lord Kraken failed to learn Mr. Ludo's secrets?" I ask. "In the end?"

Mrs. Fossil nods.

"As he grew old, the admiral lost interest. Without the head, the machine was no good, I suppose. Felix was left to tinker on alone. After His Lordship's death, Felix began working on his own projects, making models and machines out of the remains of Mr. Ludo's clockwork wonders. This is what led him to create the first waxwork figures. The Kraken family saw no harm in any of this and so, in time, Festergrimm's Eerie Waxworks was born."

"But something happened," says Vi. "Something that explains why you are Eerie-on-Sea's one-and-only professional beachcomber and not the manager of a creepy waxworks gallery."

Mrs. F gives Violet a sad smile.

"To explain that," she says, "you have to know about the pirate's treasure chest."

"What pirate's chest?"

"The one where Felix kept his secret," says Mrs. Fossil. "Because, you see, it turned out that Felix Fossil knew where the head of the robot was all along."

CHAPTER 27

FELIX FOSSIL FESSES UP

So, he *did* find it?" I blurt out. I start rummaging in the nearest basket of beachcombed knickknacks. "Where is it? Can I see it? Is it here?"

"Of course not!" Mrs. Fossil looks aghast.

"But if Felix found the head," Violet wants to know, "why didn't he tell Lord Kraken?"

Mrs. F takes a good slurp of tea and a big bite of scone, as if reinforcing herself for what's to come.

"There's always been something . . . dark," she says, brushing crumbs off her chin, "about the Krakens. And Lord Kraken was darker than most. When His Lordship ordered the parts of the destroyed robot to be gathered together, he told people to also pick up . . . to pick up . . ."

"Yes?"

". . . to pick up the exploded parts of Mr. Ludo, too."

And Vi and I can only gasp at that.

"I know," says Mrs. Fossil faintly. "Felix was ordered to bring those . . . those *grisly things* to the workshop, too. And when work began to reassemble the metal giant . . ."

"I think I see," says Violet, in a whisper.

"Oh, he shouldn't have done it!" Mrs. Fossil wails. "But he did. Lord Kraken said there was something more than mere clockwork in Mr. Ludo's wonders, something that drove and motivated the robot to search for little Pandora. He believed that something came from the inventor himself. Whatever Felix thought of this, he was too caught up in enthusiasm to object. He helped Lord Kraken rebuild the robot using bits of . . . bits of *Mr. Ludo's dead body*. It was monstrous! And our Felix was part of it."

"But the head, Mrs. F," I say. "What about the head? And the gyroscopic regulator inside it?"

"Herbie, I don't know about any gyro-thingy," says the beachcomber, with a *PARP* into a sandy handkerchief. "All I know is, when people asked Felix years later what had really become of the head, he would just chuckle and say that it was locked away safe in Purple Pimm's chest, like all the best treasures. But if he did keep the head for himself, then that makes him no better than Lord Kraken!"

And the beachcomber puts her head in her hands.

"Except, wait!" says Violet, as if thinking it through. "Maybe Felix hid the head for a reason. Maybe he *didn't* like what Lord Kraken was doing, after all? Maybe Felix Fossil wanted to stop such a powerful machine, and Mr. Ludo's secrets, from falling into the wrong hands, too. *Maybe*"—here Violet snaps her fingers as if hitting on the truth—"maybe those wrong hands were the hands of Lord Kraken himself?"

Mrs. Fossil blinks, surprised by this thought.

"Oh," she says. "Oh! Violet, maybe you're right!"

"Sounds to me," Violet declares, "that Felix Fossil could actually be the hero of this story."

"Er, this is all lovely," I interrupt loudly. "And hurrah for old Felix, and all that. But I feel like maybe we're missing the main point here. Mrs. Fossil, where is the head of Festergrimm's robot *now*?"

"Oh, I don't know that, Herbie." Mrs. Fossil sighs. "No one does. Felix took that secret to his grave."

I slump back into my chair. I can't believe it!

"But surely he said *something*! What was this about a treasure chest?"

"Like I said, that was just his little joke," Mrs. Fossil explains. "Felix said the head was hidden away in the pirate's chest. And that was that."

"There's a treasure chest in the waxworks gallery," I cry. "Downstairs, surrounded by Purple Pimm's pirates! Do you think Felix meant that? Do you think Festergrimm's head could still be hidden there? Right now?"

"You aren't the first to ask, Herbie." Mrs. Fossil looks tired, like she wants to curl up and forget it all. She wipes her nose on her handkerchief again before continuing.

"Tourists loved the Eerie Waxworks," she says. "Back in the day. They loved being spooked by the mechanical figures, and there was no escaping it was super creepy in the underground gallery. But the locals kept away. They said the waxworks moved *too much*, and not in the way they were supposed to. They said they were more alive than mere machines had a right to be. And all because of the bones they said Felix had used to complete them. The *human* bones."

"Mr. Ludo," Violet whispers.

Mrs. Fossil nods, her eyes wild.

"Then," she continues, "one day—for a dare—a tourist

jumped out of the train while it was going around the waxworks and hid himself away in the shadows. He'd heard the
stories about bones and the famous missing head. He planned
to spend the night at Festergrimm's, to find out the truth."

"What happened?" I'm on the edge of my seat now. "Did he
discover anything?"

"Who can say?" Mrs. Fossil shrugs. "They found that tourist the next day, surrounded by waxwork pirates. And he was
dead—dead as wax. A look of terror frozen on his face."

Silence follows this, broken only by the whistle of sea wind
around the shop door.

"My family never recovered from the shock," Mrs. Fossil continues in a sad voice. "And Festergrimm's never opened again.
No one would dare go down there after that, and the place got
boarded up. People blamed old Felix for what happened, for using
the remains of the dead to make a tourist attraction, though
he had long since passed away by then. But his shame became
my family's shame. Eventually, when I made my Flotsamporium
here, I hid the key to Festergrimm's and tried to forget all about
my family's waxworks past. In time, everyone else forgot, too.
Until Sebastian Eels returned and stirred it all up again."

"That's awful," says Violet, patting Mrs. F's arm. "And I'm
sorry for it all, and that some crazy tourist died. But I don't see
why any of this is *your* fault, Wendy."

"But . . ." Mrs. Fossil gulps, "but *Felix*. And . . . and the *bones*!"

"It's a strange story," Violet admits, "and it's pretty gruesome. But did anyone actually *see* any bones?"

"Well," Mrs. F blinks, "I can't say that they did, but . . ."

"You really can't be blamed for the rumors people spread about your family before you were even born," Violet says. "It's not fair."

"Everyone loves you, Mrs. F," I add, because it's true. "Except Sebastian Eels, perhaps. But that's a *good* sign."

"Sebastian says he'll write a book about us," says Mrs. Fossil, with a squeak of fright, "about how the Fossil family made money from the dead! He says I have to tell him where Festergrimm's head is hidden if I want to stop it."

"Oh, let him write his stupid book!" says Vi. "There's no way it'll be as good as my dad's. And Eels can't bully you, Wendy. I won't allow it."

"You won't?"

"*We* won't," I say.

What I don't add is that there's something else we've got to stop him from doing first. As I glance at Violet, I see that she's thinking it, too. We've got to stop Eels from finding the head of Festergrimm's robot. And the only way to do that is for Violet and me to find it first.

CHAPTER 28

THE TREASURE CHEST
OF PURPLE PIMM

D redging up all these memories has severely shaken Mrs. Fossil, so after our conversation we spend some time helping her wash up from the tea and scones, and generally trying to make everything seem as normal as possible. It's only when she's back to her usual, beachcomby self that we make our excuses and leave.

Outside it's getting dark, and the square is empty. The light bulbs on the Festergrimm's sign, flickering and buzzing in the blustery late afternoon, somehow only make the waxworks gallery seem creepier than ever. And from somewhere deep below us, we can hear the steady *cling* and *clang* of Sebastian Eels hard at work.

"I can't imagine Mrs. Fossil running a place like that," I say. "I reckon she's had a lucky escape."

"Yes, me too," Violet replies. "But how are we going to get back in there now? Look at it!"

I'm already looking. The carpenters have done a first-rate job fixing up the building, and every door and window is now bolted and reinforced. I can't see any way to get in.

"Unless there really is a secret tunnel to the waxworks gallery," she adds, "from Lord Kraken's house. Let me guess—that's the hotel, isn't it?"

"Yup," I reply. "Originally it was the Kraken's ancestral home. If there is a tunnel, it could still be there."

"But how will we find it?" Violet asks. "Do you know the way, puss?"

This last question was addressed to Erwin. But the bookshop cat, as he often does, has long since melted away into the dusk.

"Let's go back to the hotel anyway," I say. "At least with Eels busy in here, he won't pester me in my Lost-and-Foundery. And we need time to come up with one of your plans."

⚙

Back in the hotel lobby, I decide to be as conspicuous as possible, so Mr. Mollusc sees me on duty. Amber Griss, sitting at Reception, is looking bored and polishing her specs, so I stroll over.

"Hi, Amber," I say, nodding to her glasses. "Does old Mollusc Face become any prettier when you clean those?"

Amber grins.

"I bet he looks his best when you don't wear them at all," I add.

"Ha!" Amber laughs, but quickly covers it with her hand. "Herbie, don't get me into trouble," she whispers. "*Mr.* Mollusc is in one of his moods. You should watch out."

"Speaking of watching out," I reply, leaning on the desk, "what about that Sebastian Eels, eh? I know we get some dodgy guests this time of year, but what a shock seeing him again!"

"Oh, he's not so bad," Amber says, smiling to herself and tucking her hair behind one ear. "He's quite nice when you get to know him. And it's good to have Sebastian . . . I mean, Mr. Eels back again. The town has missed him."

"Is it?" I say, the smile on my face going stale. "*Has* it?"

"What's the matter, Herbie?" says Amber. "You look like you've stepped in something unfortunate."

"Oh, I was just wondering about Mr. Eels," I reply. "You know, hoping he's comfortable here. Have you seen much of him at all? Seen, for example, where he goes? In the hotel, I mean? And if, um, he uses the front door much?"

"That's an odd thing to ask." Amber places her spectacles back on her nose and turns their severe lenses onto me. "I haven't seen him go out through the front doors at all today, since you ask, though I'm not sure what business it is of yours."

I do a shrug of thanks. Then I glide backward away from the desk, like it's nothing at all. And probably it wouldn't be, if I didn't bump straight into something knobbly and unexpected, right behind me.

"Herbert Lemon," says the peevish voice of Mr. Mollusc.

I gulp.

How long has *he* been there?

"Why are you asking about our very important guest?" the manager asks in a dangerously quiet voice. "I trust you returned to him the lost item he wanted?"

"Er," I squeak, "well, the thing is . . ."

"Because if I find you have been avoiding him"—Mr. Mollusc steps forward, backing me into the reception desk—"if I find you have been avoiding doing your *job* . . ."

I clutch my cap and feel the shape of Clermit hidden inside.

"I will demote you to Toilet Brush Boy and make you scrub every bowl and pipe in the hotel! *Is that clear?*"

"Clear as spectacles, sir!" I say. "I mean, clear as toilet bowls. I *mean*, clear as clockwork. *Sir!*"

And I duck around the manager and hurry back to my Lost-and-Foundery while I still can.

"Better still," Mr. Mollusc calls after me, "I'll make you the toilet *brush*!"

I jump onto the chair in my cubbyhole and start polishing my bell. I'm still there five minutes later, when there is a *ting* from the hotel elevator.

Sebastian Eels emerges into the lobby.

I duck down. Through the crack where my desk flips open, I watch him cross the marble floor to Reception, where he orders a meal to be sent up to his room. Eels is not wearing his leather apron, but his sleeves are still rolled up, and you can tell he's been up to his elbows in melted wax and oily metalwork all day. Then he returns to the elevator. The doors slide shut behind him, and I watch the little indicator above them count the elevator's journey up to his room.

The Eel has returned to his lair.

I flip my sign to CLOSED and slip down to join Violet in my basement. Because I've just had an intriguing thought.

$$\ast\mathbf{O}\ast$$

"Are you sure?" says Violet, after I've explained what I've just seen and heard.

"Sure as I can be," I reply. "I think Sebastian Eels is using the hotel elevator to get down to the waxworks gallery. That's where Lord Kraken's secret passage must be."

"But there isn't a button marked 'secret passage' in the elevator . . ." Violet starts to say, then her eyes go wide as she remembers. *"The secret buttons!"*

And that's it. There *are* secret buttons hidden in the control panel of the elevator at the Grand Nautilus Hotel. What if Sebastian Eels knows about them, too?

"And do you remember," I continue, "during that business with Gargantis, how I made a mistake and revealed a button marked 'Laboratory.'"

"I do!" Violet throws down her book and leaps up. "We didn't know what it was back then, but that must be Lord Kraken's clockwork laboratory! *That's* how we'll get back into the wax-works! Herbie, you are a genius. Come on!"

Now, don't get me wrong, I like all this talk of me being a genius. Being called a genius is *great*! But the problem is, I have to spoil the moment by explaining to Violet that actually, while I know how to reveal *some* of the secret buttons, I don't know the code for one marked "Laboratory."

"I found it by accident, remember?"

"But . . ." Violet pauses, her mind whirring like crazy. "But if you know some of the codes—like how to get to Lady Kraken's floor and to the attic—why don't you know them all?"

"Vi, I'm not supposed to know *any* of them," I say. "I only know some because Mr. Mollusc has a list of them pinned up on the wall in his office. One day, for something to do while he was shouting at me, I memorized a few."

"Well, then, Herbert Lemon," says Violet. "There's only one thing to do: you're going to have to go back to the manager's office right now and memorize the rest. Because with Eels safely in his room for the night and the coast clear, we have no time to waste!"

CHAPTER 29

LEMON HERBIE

Have you ever eaten a Lemon Cream Delight? I think you'd know if you had. The only place in the world you can get an authentic Lemon Cream Delight is the Grand Nautilus Hotel in Eerie-on-Sea, and even then Chef only bakes them on Saturdays. It's a teatime delicacy that people travel miles to eat, sitting in the hotel dining room, looking out over the sea, with dreamy looks on their faces as they chew.

They are *heavenly* lemony.

They are creamy *delights*!

Oh, and they are more commonly known as Lemon Herbies, because—believe it or not—the Lemon Cream Delight was invented in my honor.

At least, that's what I've been told. Chef created the first Lemon Herbie, or so the story goes, shortly after I arrived in Eerie-on-Sea, washed up in my crate of lemons. They even say he still uses the very same lemons I arrived with to this day, which explains the mysterious tang of ocean in the Lemon Cream Delight that people go wild for.

But that's just what they say.

Because even though I'm told the Lemon Herbie was created to celebrate me, I never get to actually eat one. And *that's* because the only say that matters around here is Mr. Mollusc's say, and Mr. Mollusc says that "it's all poppycock and nonsense!" and that "Lemon Cream Delights are too expensive to be leftovers," and, "Anyway, they're far too good for annoying little shrimps like *you*, Herbert Lemon."

Despite all this, as I head across the hotel lobby toward the kitchen, I can't help thinking that, as it's Saturday today, maybe— *just maybe*—my plate of evening leftovers might include a spare Lemon Herbie.

I haven't forgotten my mission to get the secret-button codes from Mr. Mollusc's office, by the way. It's just that after everything that's happened recently, I'll need a really rock-solid excuse to be out from behind my desk if the manager sees me now. But even Mr. Mollusc can't stop me from collecting my evening meal at the appointed time.

I head around behind the reception desk and into the staff corridor that leads to the kitchen. About halfway down is the door to Mr. Mollusc's office. It's slightly open, but I hurry by.

On its usual shelf near the bins in the shouty, steamy kitchen, my evening plate is waiting. There is yesterday's potato salad, a humorously shaped banana I'm not surprised the guests don't want, cold runner beans, a few of those mini-quiche things that Violet likes, and two very hard croissants.

"Bon appétit, Herbie," says a kitchen assistant, hurrying past with a heap of dishes. Beyond him, other kitchen staff are chopping, frying, and running around as Chef—enormous and unapproachable at the heart of the kitchen—bellows at everyone in French.

"Thanks," I say, taking my plate. "Um, any Lemon Herbies left, at all? By any chance?"

The kitchen assistant gives me a regretful look of disbelief that I would even ask such a ridiculous question. Then he plunges his dishes in the sink. Disappointed but not surprised, I stroll back out of the kitchen with my dinner, such as it is.

I slow down as I head back toward the manager's office. The door being slightly open is a good sign; Mr. Mollusc likes to hang around in the dining room at mealtimes, fussing over the guests and helping himself to food when he thinks no one is looking. The elevator codes are on a tatty old slip of paper pinned to a corkboard behind his desk, so this should be a quick in-and-out job.

I stop, holding my plate of leftovers ostentatiously—in case I'm caught—and quietly push the door open a little . . .

And freeze.

Because Mr. Mollusc is in there!

He's standing behind the desk, his back to the door, pouring himself a large glass of something from a bottle I recognize as coming from Lady Kraken's private cellar.

I go into immediate emergency reverse gear and begin back-pedaling out of there.

But then I freeze again.

Because there, on Mr. Mollusc's desk—sitting on a china plate in all its unmistakable sugary glory—is a Lemon Cream Delight.

A Lemon Herbie!

And suddenly I understand why there is never, *ever* one left over.

Mr. Mollusc claims them first!

The manager stops pouring and starts putting the cork back in the bottle.

I have about 12.5 nanoseconds to decide what to do.

But, before my brain can come to any decisions, my body starts moving anyway. I crouch swiftly beneath the desk, fighting to stop potato salad and rude banana from sliding onto the floor.

What are you doing? my brain demands to know, but my body doesn't answer. I have a feeling the decision to hide was actually made by my stomach, but my stomach is whistling and pretending it didn't hear the question.

"Ah!" says Mr. Mollusc to himself, sitting down at his desk and sipping from his glass. I have to scrunch over to one side— my plate tipping at crazy angles—to avoid getting his knees in my face. "Her Ladyship keeps a good sherry, but I deserve it after the day I've had. And now for this little beauty . . ."

And I hear him pick up a silver cake fork.

I knock on the underside of the desk.

Three hard raps.

What? my brain gasps, starting to freak out, but my stomach seems to have staged an insurrection and put my body under new management.

Knock, knock, knock! I go again.

"Oh, who's there?" Mr. Mollusc demands, slamming the cake fork down. "Just come in, why don't you? The door is open."

He thinks someone is knocking at the door!

See? my stomach tells my stupefied brain as I knock again.

"Oh, for heaven's sake!" Mollusc snaps. "Leave me in peace, whoever you are!"

Knock.

KNOCK.

KNOCK!

go my knuckles, and Mollusc scrapes his chair back and leaps to his feet. He storms over to the door and flings it fully open.

"What?" he demands.

But, of course, the corridor is empty.

And it's now that my stomach issues a series of urgent orders to the rest of my body that even my brain is going to have to admit are pretty impressive.

First, I rise up silently on the other side of the desk, balancing the plate on one hand. Then I smartly tug the sheet of paper with the codes right off the corkboard. Finally, I slip the paper under my cap and duck back beneath the desk, just as Mollusc—muttering about pranksters—strides around the desk and plops himself back into his chair.

But now there's a new problem: Mr. Mollusc has closed the door behind him!

Knock-knock-knock-knock-knock . . .

I go on the underside of the desk, in some desperation.

. . . knock-knock-knock-KNOCK!

The manager leaps back up, runs to the door, and nearly pulls it off its hinges.

"Caught you!" he cries. "Oh . . ."

Of course, there is *still* no one there.

"Come back here!" the furious Mr. Mollusc shouts, running down the corridor toward the hotel lobby, determined to catch the prankster red-handed.

Meanwhile the prankster—which is me, obviously—rises up from under the desk once more, tips one of the hard, old croissants off my leftovers plate and onto Mr. Mollusc's, and slides the Lemon Herbie the other way.

Then I step out into the corridor, straighten my Lost-and-Founder's cap, and hurry back toward the lobby and the safety of my cubbyhole. My brain and my stomach are both holding their breath (if you see what I mean) because, amazingly, I seem to be getting away with this!

Except that's when Mr. Mollusc reappears.

He fills the corridor ahead, his eyes bulging with fury as he sees me approach.

"Hello again, sir," I manage to say without a squeak, strolling toward the manager with my plate of leftovers in my hands, like everything is fine. But I know that if Mr. Mollusc spots the Lemon Herbie sitting on top of my potato salad, I'll be done for.

My boggled brain—seeing disaster unfold—finally catches up with the situation, pushes my stomach back to where it belongs, and urgently switches on my most annoying grin, at full beam. This is the grin I use when the manager accuses me of something but I have a good excuse he can't argue against. It always makes the vein throb on his forehead.

"Herbert Lemon!" Mr. Mollusc spits out my name, too busy glaring at my grinning face to examine my plate. "Did *you* knock on my door?"

"I can honestly say I didn't, sir," I reply, gliding past him. "I was too busy thinking about your little speech in the railway station yesterday morning. The one about the universe dishing out rewards and everyone getting their just deserts? You're so *wise*, sir. Good night!"

And with this I stroll down the corridor, calm as a whole bucket of cucumbers, even though inside I'm *ping*ing with fright.

I cross the vast marble floor of the hotel lobby, not yet daring to breathe. But the hotel manager doesn't come after me. My brain and my stomach do a high five (so to speak), and in no time I'm back through the cubbyhole of my Lost-and-Foundery and running down the steps to the safety of my cellar.

CHAPTER 30

MORE SECRET BUTTONS

I can't believe you have a cake named after you!" says Violet as I divide the Lemon Herbie into two and give her half.

"According to Mr. Mollusc, I haven't," I reply. "The manager said I'm only allowed to eat one on my birthday."

Violet bites into the heavenly cake, and her eyes go dreamy and far away. A blissful, lemony silence descends over the two of us as we chomp together, though I swear I can hear angels singing somewhere.

"Delicious!" Violet says eventually, letting Erwin lick the cream off her fingers. "But wait, Herbie. Your birthday? I don't even know when that is."

"Neither do I," I say. "Nor does anyone else. Shipwrecked in

Eerie-on-Sea with no memory, remember? No birthday for me."

"Herbie," Violet says, "that's really sad. I'm sorry."

"No need." I shrug, pushing the plate to one side. There is only one hard croissant left on it. Neither of us fancy that now, so Violet slips it into her coat pocket for later. "Now that dinner is taken care of," I say, changing the subject, "let's get down to business."

I pull out the code sheet that explains how to uncover the secret buttons in the hotel elevator.

"I've never even heard of half these places," I say, reading down the list of hidden destinations. "Ice cellar, shooting gallery, ballroom . . . we have a *ballroom*?"

"Whoever built the hotel made good use of the tunnels and passages beneath the town," says Violet. "But here's what we want," she adds, tapping the paper. "Laboratory."

And beside it is the combination of buttons you have to press on the elevator's control panel to make that particular secret button appear.

"No one built it to be a hotel," I say. "It was the Kraken family's home first, remember? It's amazing to think Lord Kraken's lab has been down there all this time, without anyone knowing."

"Eels knew," says Vi. "And for all we know, Lady Kraken still goes down to the ballroom from time to time, or the shooting gallery to practice with her pistols. I'm sure she has pistols. And even Mr. Mollusc must have been curious about these hidden places. But how did Eels find out?"

"Two slippery creatures may live in the same slimy pool," says a feline voice, and we look up to see Erwin wiping his whiskers and pretending not to be paying attention.

"It would make sense for Mollusc to help Eels out," I agree, nodding. "I think that Mr. Mollusc probably knows more about the real Eels than anyone."

"No matter." Violet is on her feet again and pulling on her coat. "We have no time to waste. Bring your flashlight, Herbie. Thanks to you, we have a chance to find the missing head of Festergrimm's robot and be safely back here before Sebastian Eels even gets up in the morning."

⚙❁

By now the hotel has become quiet, and the lobby is empty. Amber Griss is away from her desk when I lead Violet and Erwin out from my cubbyhole. In the gleaming hotel elevator, I wait till the doors have slid shut before turning to the dimpled keypad and its six visible buttons.

"Exciting!" says Violet, looking far brighter and more cheerful about things than seems sensible.

"Is it?" I reply. "Last time we were down in the waxworks gallery, we saw horrors. Actual horrors! And I was nearly skewered by a mad author with a trident."

"Yes, but Eels won't be there now." Violet takes the code paper from me. "All we have to do is see if the missing head really is in the pirate's treasure chest and take it. Sebastian Eels will be defeated without even knowing it."

With these brave words, Violet presses four of the elevator buttons at the same time. There is an electronic whirring, and a new button appears in a decorative dimple on the brass panel:

−3 LABORATORY.

Violet jabs this with her finger, and immediately the elevator begins to descend.

"Unless Eels has already found the head," I reply. "What then?"

But Violet doesn't have an answer to that.

The elevator gives a small bump and hiss as it arrives. The lights flicker, and it definitely feels like we've reached an underground floor that is rarely used.

Then the doors slide slowly open.

To reveal darkness.

I switch on my flashlight and shine it into a crumbly, brick-lined corridor.

"Lord Kraken's secret passage," I whisper. "We've found it!"

"It looks like part of the Netherways," Violet whispers back as she steps out. Erwin follows her, twitching his whiskers. "Have you been here before, puss?"

"Na-ow," meows the cat.

"Let's get this over with," I mutter, bringing up the rear.

With a clack, the elevator doors close behind us, and the comforting world of the Grand Nautilus Hotel disappears. I suddenly realize I have no idea how to call the elevator carriage back if we need to make a quick getaway.

"Come on, Herbie!" Violet calls, already striding ahead and making me jog to catch up. After a few twists and turns, the tunnel ends at a metal door. The door has a keyhole in it, shaped like a gargoyle with an open mouth.

"This looks really old," Violet says, admiring the pitted iron surface. "It's time to wind up Clermit. We'll need him to pick the lock."

"I, er, I forgot to bring his winder key," I admit. "Again."

"Oh, Herbie!" Violet rolls her eyes, twisting the iron ring above the keyhole in exasperation. "How are going to . . . ?"

But she stops speaking when the door creaks open.

"It's unlocked?" I gasp.

"Eels must be pretty confident," Violet replies.

I'm not so sure. It doesn't seem right that he'd leave the door unlocked, but Violet is already entering the room and pulling down a brass switch on the wall to activate the lights. A string of electric bulbs of differing strengths crackle and fizz into life, to reveal a sight that takes my breath away.

THE CLOCKWORK
LABORATORY

The room is vast. In fact, *room* isn't the right word; it's a cavern.

A cavern easily the size of the hotel lobby, hidden deep underground and filled with wonderful, clockworky things.

"Also very grubby, *cobwebby* things," Violet says, but I'm too busy running my hand over the brass armatures, fly-sprocket repeaters, and cogs by the basket-load. There is a long work desk in the middle of the cavern, covered in contraptions and parts, and on one wall is a vast arrangement of nails and hooks, on which are hung every tool you can imagine.

"This is amazing!" I say, staring up at the wall of tools and feeling my cap slip back down my head. "And there, in the corner!" I add, pointing to the lower edge of the tool wall where two letters have been carefully chiseled.

"F.F.," Violet reads aloud. "Is that . . . ?"

"Felix Fossil," I say. "This must be where he worked, all those years, first as Lord Kraken's assistant, then on his own."

"Prrp!" says Erwin, and we turn to find the bookshop cat is pulling something from a box on the work desk.

"A bird!" Violet exclaims as we see what it is. "A windup bird!"

Sure enough, clutched in Erwin's teeth is a beautiful and intricate clockwork bird, made of tarnished silver, with a golden beak.

"It's smashed, though," I say, taking the poor thing in my hands. "Someone has pulled out its workings."

"Eels?" Violet suggests.

"Or Felix," I reply. "Or Lord Kraken. Or maybe even Ludo Festergrimm himself, when he built the robot to find his daughter. Everything here looks like it has been junked. Taken to pieces for parts and left to decay."

Beside the box is a large parchment, which I start to unroll. I gasp when I see what's on it and quickly unroll it in full, right along the length of the desk. Soon, spread out in the buzzing, uncertain light of the laboratory is the blueprint of a giant clockwork man, in excruciatingly cool detail.

"Bladderwracks!" I hiss under my breath, tracing my finger along the plans. "The robot!"

"But where is it?" says Violet, looking around. "The machine itself?"

There is a large moth-eaten curtain hanging over the wall opposite the tools. Violet peers behind it.

"I don't think we'll find the actual robot, Vi," I reply, still gazing deeply into the diagram. "Worst luck. I bet it was recycled into the skeletons of the waxworks, like the rest of Mr. Ludo's clockwork wonders."

"Herbie . . ." Violet says, still looking behind the curtain, but I haven't finished yet.

"And Sebastian Eels couldn't reassemble Festergrimm's robot in just a couple of days, Vi, even if he could find all the parts."

"Herbie!" Violet says, more urgently this time.

Erwin joins her at the curtain and goes "Phsss!"

"No, the robot itself will be long gone," I continue, tormenting myself with mind's-eye visions of the great bronze machine that I must accept I'll never get to see for myself. "I hate to say it, Vi, but we'll be lucky if we can find even the head after all this time. And besides . . ."

With an immense heave, Violet sweeps back the curtain, cutting my words short. The centuries-old fabric tears, and the whole thing falls to the ground in a cloud of dust.

I stop speaking, the rest of my words falling silently from

my mouth and rolling away across the floor. Slowly I raise the flashlight, its narrow beam trembling out from my hand as I sweep it up and up to illuminate the huge *thing* that Violet has revealed, standing in a double-decker-size recess off the main chamber.

I sink to the floor in shock and awe.

Because there—looming over us in the secret cavern— stands the battered bronze body of a giant metal man.

⚙O✿

"Festergrimm!" I say when I can finally form real words again. "Festergrimm's robot!"

The machine is surrounded by wooden scaffolding and work platforms. A large panel is open in the giant's metal chest, and despite the fur of dust, I can pick out the gleam of brass parts within. The outer plates of the bronze colossus, tarnished green with age and neglect, look slightly misshapen, as if they have been beaten back into shape after some great explosion. Which, of course, they were—if the legend is true.

"I had no idea," whispers Violet, "it would be so *big*."

Erwin leaps up the scaffolding—ascending in cat jumps— and scampers until he gets to the top. Between the metal giant's shoulders protrudes a stubby tube that must be his neck. And above this, where the head should be, is nothing but empty space.

"The breastplate is open," says Violet, standing next to me now. "Do you think Eels has actually been working on it?"

I look up at the exposed workings. There is an odd-shaped gap in the clockwork, but everything is so dusty, it's hard to be sure of anything from down here.

"It doesn't look like it has been touched since Felix's time," I say, straightening my cap. "Besides, the part of the robot Eels is really interested in is the one part that isn't here: the head."

"All this," says Violet, raising her arms at the great bronze robot, "to find a missing girl. And still, she was never found."

I feel another twang in my brain at these words. And that's a weird thing to feel in your brain, isn't it? A twang? But how else do I describe it? The sad fate of lost Pandora Festergrimm touches me in some way, though it's impossible to see why it should. I shake the twang away and begin to climb the scaffolding after Erwin.

"Herbie?" says Violet. "What are you doing?"

"Getting a closer look," I reply.

"We have something to do, Herbie," Violet reminds me, pointing to a wooden door at the other end of the cavern that we haven't explored yet, "and we need to hurry up and do it, while the coast is clear."

I stop climbing. Violet has a point. But before I can reply, we hear a sound, clear as day: the sound of a mechanism that hasn't moved for centuries, creaking ever so slightly.

CHAPTER 32

PIRATE TREASURE

D id you hear that?" Violet asks me.

"I didn't do it!" I squeak, letting go of the scaffolding.

Then we both look at the still-as-a-statue metal giant.

"Erwin, was that you?" I call up the scaffolding to where I last saw the cat.

"Naow!" comes a sound from behind us. Erwin is sitting on the ground, his ice-blue eyes enormous with alarm. It—whatever *it* was—clearly wasn't him.

"We need to get a move on," Violet says, whispering again. "Come on, Herbie."

So, with a fearful glance behind us at Festergrimm's long-dead bronze robot, we open the wooden door.

Behind it is another, smaller chamber, and this one we recognize.

"It's the murder room!" I squeak, seeing the body parts hanging around, the glass eyes, and the things in jars that we saw yesterday, back when we first discovered Eels at work in the waxworks gallery.

"Don't call it that, Herbie," says Violet, looking disturbed. "This is just the place where the waxworks themselves were made. And are now *un*made," she adds, looking around at the destruction left by Sebastian Eels. "But that means the main gallery, with the exhibits and the train track, must be just through there." She points to yet another door—the very door we were caught peering around yesterday, when Eels came after us.

We tiptoe through the wreckage—between pools of melted wax, chopped limbs, and singed wigs—and down the short corridor beyond, until we reach the last door.

Pushing it open, we look out into the subterranean waxworks gallery.

"Doesn't look too different," says Violet, as I flick the flashlight around.

Sure enough, the mermaids and mad monks and mythological beasties are still standing around awkwardly, their heads lolling, their clothes barely holding together. Between them runs the narrow track of the little train, looping here and there between the waxy horrors. And standing over it all, like the King of Make-Believe, is the model of Festergrimm's robot, looking feeble and ridiculous now that we have seen the real thing.

"The treasure chest is over *there*," Violet whispers, turning my wandering flashlight arm in the right direction.

A knot of grotesque pirates—Purple Pimm's crew, at a guess—are standing in a crystal grotto, guarding the very treasure chest we hid behind yesterday. I can't help remembering Mrs. Fossil's story about the tourist who once spent the night down here and was discovered the next day, surrounded by these terrible figures.

Terrified to death.

As if sensing the return of my queasy feeling, Violet takes the flashlight from me and leads the way over to the pirates. She peers close into the face of one of them, the light glinting off his fake gold teeth and single remaining glass eye.

"What's the story of this dread Captain Pimm, anyway?" she asks.

"Like the doc says," I explain, "she turned against the king back in sixteen hundred and something and stole a ship. She and her fearsome crew caused havoc across the Caribbean, stealing the king's gold. Eventually she returned to Eerie-on-Sea, to hide her vast treasure in the bay. There's a legend that one of the islands in Maw Rocks is actually hollow and that Purple Pimm's gold is hidden in a crystal cave inside. But no one knows which one, and so the treasure is still out there. Somewhere."

"Well, we're here for treasure of a different kind." Violet turns her back on the pirates and shines the flashlight down onto the treasure chest. The lid is firmly shut. "If what Mrs. Fossil says is true, and not just a joke, then this chest may well contain Festergrimm's head."

"The head of his robot, you mean," I say, eager to make the correction. "But what if the other things Mrs. Fossil told us are also true? Maybe there is more than waxworks down here."

And I do a gulp.

Violet looks annoyed.

"Herbie, do you honestly think there are bits of real dead body down here? In the waxworks?"

"This is Eerie-on-Sea, Violet," is my only reply.

Vi ignores me and reaches out to flip open the chest. But if she's hoping to silence me by revealing what's inside, she's disappointed: the lid is firmly shut.

"We did see it opening and closing, though," I say, tugging at the lid myself, but with no luck, "when we went around on the train, remember? It was all costume jewelry and fake gold inside."

"Yeah, but right now," Violet says through a grunt, heaving at the lid with both hands, "we can't even get *that* . . . *gngn.*"

But it's no good. Even when Violet's strength is combined with the might of an official Lost-and-Founder, we just can't get the chest open at all.

"Four hands may be better than two," calls a feline voice from across the gallery, "but sometimes all you need is a finger."

We turn, and the beam of Violet's flashlight lands on Erwin, who is sitting beside the open control panel we saw Eels use yesterday to start the ghost train. He's twitching his whiskers at the buttons.

"Of course!" Vi heads over to the cat. "We need to turn the power on and let the chest open by itself. Herbie, get ready," she calls back to me. "Shout when it's open enough!"

And Violet presses the green button.

The waxwork exhibits spring into life all around us. Lights the color of deep-sea phosphorescence flicker on, the faces of the fearsome mermaids glow as if underwater, and clouds of vapor roll out, lit up like sea mist in eerie moonlight. The gallery fills with the ghost train wail and the waxwork pirates judder, moving their eyes as they turn their heads, and the treasure chest starts to open.

A heap of jewels and treasure is revealed within the chest, bathing my face in golden light.

I wave my arms in the air and shout.

"Now, Vi! It's open enough now!"

Violet jabs the red button, and as suddenly as they started, the waxwork figures shudder to a halt. The spectacle lights wink out, and we're plunged into darkness again.

"Er, Vi?" I squeak, suddenly finding myself alone in the invisible presence of Purple Pimm's vile crew! "Vi, where are you?"

I feel something.

A cold, dead something, that flops onto my shoulder.

"Vi!"

Soon the beam of the flashlight is bobbing back to me and shining in my face.

"Herbie? Herbie, what's wrong?" comes Violet's voice from behind the light.

I lift one trembling hand and point at the thing on my shoulder.

Then I turn my head, slowly, and dare to look.

It's a hand.

A flubbery waxwork pirate hand, clutching at my shoulder.

Where it had landed *after* the power went out!

I see that the waxwork pirate who owns the hand, whose wig has slipped and who has lost both waxwork ears, is staring right at me.

"Argh!" I cry, leaping away and almost knocking Violet over.

"It's nothing, Herbie," says Violet. "The waxworks are falling apart, that's all."

"Can we just grab the head and get out of here, please?" I reply. "The sooner we're back up in my Lost-and-Foundery, with the doors locked and all the lights on, the better!"

Violet and I return to the treasure chest, locked now in an open position. Up close, the fakeness of the jewels and treasure is even more obvious.

"Hold the flashlight, Herbie," says Violet, rolling up her sleeve.

"What are you going to do?" I ask, but she's already doing it: Violet has plunged her arm into the pantomime bling, up to her elbow, and is groping around in it.

"I think . . ." she says. "Yes, I think . . ."

"What?" I reply. *"What?"*

"I think . . . something is there. Something . . . big. Something . . ."

Violet pulls hard on the thing she's found, bringing it up in a cascade of phony pirate treasure. She holds it up to the flashlight beam.

It's a human skull.

CHAPTER 33

BLUNDERBUSS

estergrimm's head!" I gasp, the words almost not coming out at all. "Ludo Festergrimm's actual *head*!"

Violet looks profoundly shocked. She holds the skull and stares at it, like in that Shakespeare play where someone holds a skull and stares at it.

"Bladderwracks!" she says eventually, borrowing my word for the occasion, but I don't mind—I couldn't have put it better myself! Have we got this all completely wrong? Is this grisly skull the object that Felix Fossil hid all those years ago? Is *this* what that nosy tourist found, alone in the dark, all those years later? But then, just as I'm expecting Violet to gently place the skull back in the chest, with great reverence for the dead, she blinks at it. And then she leans in really close and peers into its eye socket.

"Wait a minute . . ." she says.

"A *whole* minute?" I reply. "Do we have to?"

Violet raps on the skull with one disrespectful knuckle.

Toc, toc, toc.

"I don't think there's anyone in, Vi," I whisper. "Not anymore."

"There never was," Violet says then, tossing the skull to me. "It's made of *plaster*, Herbie. It's fake! Like everything else down here."

I catch the skull, only just managing not to drop my flashlight.

"Plaster?" I say, turning the grinning, bony head this way and that in the light, and seeing that Violet is right. "So, does that mean . . . ?" I say. "Does that mean . . . wait, what *does* that mean? That Felix Fossil *didn't* find the head of Festergrimm's robot, after all? That's it's still out there somewhere?"

"Not necessarily," Vi replies. "It just means it wasn't hidden in Purple Pimm's treasure chest. It could have been left in some other hiding place, and the secret never told. But is that likely? Would Felix have wanted such a vital part of the robot to stay hidden forever?"

I hold the skull up and look it straight in the eye socket.

I think back over what Mrs. Fossil told us, and about the strange and tragic story of Mr. Ludo and his missing daughter.

I think of the great clockwork giant waiting incomplete in the chamber nearby, and the detailed plans laid out on the worktable.

Something starts to niggle.

"Herbie?" I hear Violet's voice say, but I tune her out. I've seen something and not noticed it. I *know* I have. But . . . what?

Then, with a thunderclap of realization, I suddenly get it.

"Vi!" I cry. "The head. It's not in the pirate's treasure chest. And yet, *it is*, at the same time. Oh, clever old Felix Fossil—I know where to find the head of Festergrimm's robot!"

"You do?" says Violet.

"You do?" says another voice that no one is expecting. "Well, about time. I was beginning to think I'd made a mistake allowing you two back down here."

And Sebastian Eels steps out of the shadows and points an enormous gun at us.

"You!" Violet gasps.

"Yes, me," says Eels. "Who did you expect? The ghost of Ludo Festergrimm? Now, you were saying, Herbert Lemon? About the head?"

"Um!" I gasp, my brain struggling to adjust to this sudden turn of events. "I . . . I know nothing!"

"I bet that old pop gun isn't even loaded!" Violet declares, pointing at the bizarre weapon in the writer's hands. "It looks as old and clapped out as you are."

Sebastian Eels gives a sickly grin and hefts the gun.

"Say what you like," he replies, "but they don't make double-barreled blunderbusses like this anymore. It belonged to Lord Kraken himself, a man after my own heart. He was looking for the deepest secret, too, you know, and spared no expense. This gun is a fine weapon, Violet Parma, and I've been itching for an excuse to test it out."

With that, Sebastian Eels swings the blunderbuss around, points it at a nearby waxwork pirate, and pulls the trigger.

There is an almighty explosion.

A ferocious plume of fire erupts from one barrel of the gun.

The pirate is obliterated—carried away in a hail of white-hot metal shot and spattered across the whole of the gallery. Violet and I are left cowering in terror, clutching Erwin.

"Hell's teeth!" gasps Sebastian Eels, who struggled to stay on his feet with the recoil. He gazes in adoration at the smoke rising from the barrel. "Now *that's* a weapon. I could stop a charging rhino with this, so I can certainly wipe out a couple of annoying little sand fleas like you two."

And he turns the blunderbuss back toward us, its second barrel still loaded.

"Hands up!" snaps Eels. "And get talking!"

I look at Violet. She looks at me. Then we both look at Erwin.

We put our hands up, which means Erwin is released. He jumps down and vanishes into the dark. But Eels clearly isn't interested in bookshop cats.

"What did you mean," Violet asks, as bravely as she can with a gaping barrel of death pointing at her, "when you said you *allowed* us back down here?"

"I know how these things usually go," Eels says, giving us a cold regard. "I set my plans in motion, and then you two meddling busybodies work it all out and get in my way. Well, not this time. This time you're going to work *for me.* I can't find the robot's head, but I bet that flaky beachcomber friend of yours knows more than she's letting on. All I had to do was leave the cellar door unlocked and wait for you two to show me the answer. So, out with it. What did dear old Wendy tell you?"

"Mrs. Fossil said," I reply, pointing at the nearby pirate display and the treasure, "that the missing head is in Purple Pimm's chest. And that's all she knows."

"Except, it isn't," Eels says, raising the blunderbuss as if preparing to fire. "So maybe I should count to three . . ."

"Except, *it is!*" I cry. "Just . . . just not in the way you expect. But if you stop waving that gun around, I can show you."

And so that's how Violet and I find ourselves picking our way back toward the tunnel that we descended yesterday—the one the train comes down—with Eels following behind. It's hard to walk up the railway line with our hands in the air, but somehow we manage it without tripping. I can sense the open barrel of the blunderbuss pointing straight at our backs as we begin our climb.

"When we get to the top," Violet whispers to me from inside her hair, "we can run. He can't shoot us both."

"Stop whispering!" Eels shouts. "And yes, I can."

We emerge from the tunnel and arrive once more on the ground floor of the waxworks gallery. The train is waiting at its station, opposite the counter and dusty souvenir stand. A few waxwork figures are standing around, including the dread pirate Purple Pimm, who has been wheeled back in after she was displayed in the square earlier today.

"So, where is it?" Eels demands. "My patience has run through. Tell me where the head is hidden."

"Purple Pimm has it," I say, pointing to the pirate captain, with her feathered hat and cutlass. "In her chest."

"But it's not *there* . . . !" Eels growls in fury.

Then he stops and blinks in sudden realization.

He lowers the gun, pushes Violet and me out of the way, and grabs the waxwork pirate by her frilly collar. He knocks her hat and wig to the ground, and then—with a great wrenching motion—he tears her great purple coat away, revealing a metal rib cage beneath. And within that iron framework, something huge and dark can be seen—something with a grille for a mouth, and two enormous glass lamps for eyes.

It's the head of Festergrimm's robot.

Hidden in Purple Pimm's chest!

CHAPTER 34

ON THE COUNT OF THREE

Sebastian Eels cries out in triumph. He hammers on the metal cage that forms the model pirate's chest with the butt of his blunderbuss. The iron structure—already weak and corroded with age—buckles and breaks, and the effigy of dread pirate Purple Pimm finally falls apart. Now the long-lost head of Festergrimm's giant is revealed, gleaming in greenish bronze. His lamp eyes are round and staring, and his mouth gapes behind the grille. In the flashlight beam, we can see three bells hanging there.

Eels thrusts the blunderbuss into my hands, slides his own hands between the bars of the grille, and flicks the bells with a *pang* and a *dong* and a *rang*.

"Incredible!" he whispers. "After all this time . . ."

With a grunt of effort, he lifts the head out of the ruined waxwork and holds it up for us to see.

"Behold!" he cries. "The head of Festergrimm's robot!"

"Amazing!" I gasp, despite everything.

"It is," Eels agrees in a wondering voice, "but the legends of Eerie-on-Sea never cease to amaze me. And inside the head, just waiting to be claimed, is Mr. Ludo's gyroscopic regulator."

I glance at Vi and she glances back. Then she looks down at the terrible blunderbuss in my hands. With all this amazement going on, I seem to have ended up holding the gun!

"Um," I declare. "Hands up!"

"The catch is stuck," says Sebastian Eels, ignoring me as he scrabbles uselessly at a closed metal panel on top of the bronze head. "Dammit, I'll need tools to get this open."

"Don't move!" I try again, waving the weapon about, "or . . . or . . . *I'll shoot!*"

"No," says Eels, lowering the head to the floor, "you won't."

And with that he grabs the blunderbuss, twists it out of my hands, and thumps me in the stomach with it.

"Why do you think I gave my gun to you," he explains as I sink to the ground, "and not Violet?"

"Why, you . . . !" Violet cries, finally making her move, but she's stopped in her tracks by the blunderbuss being aimed at her again. At this range she would be blasted to billions of bits. She glares furiously but has no choice but to raise her hands, as I stagger back to my feet.

"Enough chat," says Sebastian Eels. "Pick up the head. You two can carry it down to the laboratory for me. And if you try any tricks . . . well, you won't try any tricks, now, will you?"

He grins over the double barrels of his gun.

And so, Violet and I pick up the head. Well, what else can we do? There are two handles, one on either side, where ears would normally be.

"It weighs a ton!" Violet gasps as we struggle to lift it.

"Stop complaining!" Eels snaps. "Put it in the train—we'll take it down that way."

I'm feeling a bit deflated, I have to admit. We wanted to stop Eels from getting the gyroscopic regulator, but all we've done is find it for him. And how did he know I wouldn't shoot him while I had the chance? It's all very annoying. If we had tied the robot's head in a nice bow and hand-delivered it with a bunch of flowers to his hotel room, we couldn't have helped the scoundrel more.

We reach the train, but the sides of the carriages are too high for us to lift the head in.

"We'll have to swing it," says Violet, "to get it over."

"Then get swinging," Eels barks.

"On three, Herbie," Violet says, and gives me a secret wink.

I'm not entirely sure what this means, but I do know that when Violet says things like "On three, Herbie," and does a secret wink, Herbie had better spend One and Two getting ready for something unexpected.

"One . . ." says Vi, as we start the head swinging together. Then, when it falls back, we use its own weight to swing it forward again, raising the head higher still, as Violet says, "Two . . ."

"Get on with it!" yells Sebastian Eels. "I haven't got all night."

"Just one more . . ." gasps Violet. *"Three!"*

And, with an enormous effort, we raise the bronze head high enough to clear the rail, and I finally understand the plan. Instead of letting it go, we swing the head back once more, toward Eels, with all the force we can manage.

It hits the man in the stomach (or even a bit below).

"Oof!" goes Sebastian Eels, taken by surprise and dropping the blunderbuss with a clatter. He slumps down onto the ground, clutching his middle (or even a bit below). "Urgh!"

"Swing, Herbie!" Violet shouts, as together we heave the robot's head a fourth and final time, over the rail and into the train carriage. It lands on the soft cushions of the seat. We jump in beside it, and Violet reaches over to the control panel that operates the ghost train and jabs the green button.

The train bursts into life and lurches toward the tunnel.

"Come back here!" cries Sebastian Eels, struggling to his feet. He snatches up the blunderbuss.

"Herbie, get down!" Violet yells, and we drop down below the seats.

There is an almighty explosion, and the air is filled with heat and fire. The back of the metal train carriage rings like a gong and buckles inward under the force of the blast. Hundreds of nuts and bolts and cogs and washers that had been loaded in the gun ricochet crazily around us. But already Vi and I are in the tunnel, trundling past spooky fishermen and waxwork mermaids, toward the gallery below. And between us, on the seat, is the head of Festergrimm's robot.

"You can't escape!" comes the roar of Sebastian Eels from above, his voice echoing monstrously in the tunnel.

"And you can't fire again!" Violet shouts back, leaning over the buckled rear of the carriage and making rude signs in the direction of our pursuer. "So, *ha*!"

"Er, you do know guns can be reloaded, don't you?" I tell her as we rush out into the main subterranean gallery and began to wend our way around the eerie exhibits. "And this train will just bring us back round to the station."

"Which is why," Violet says, grabbing one end of the bronze head, "we're going to have to get off. Right about . . . now!"

And with a powerful heave, Violet swings the head up and

jumps out of the train, crashing into a nearby display and knocking over a waxwork smuggler.

"Herbie, help me!"

I jump out the other side and leap across the track to reach Violet. Together we get hold of the bronze head again and start lugging it toward the service door that leads to the laboratory. Without the flashlight it's hard to see, and only the flickering electric light of the waxwork dioramas shows us the way.

"Is he still following?" I ask, trying to catch sight of Eels behind us in the shadows and vapor.

"I don't think he'll give up," Violet replies as we enter the corridor and head toward the workshop. "But hopefully he'll get run over by the returning train."

I like this idea, but somehow I doubt we'll be that lucky. We hurry through the waxworks workshop—past the chopped-up body parts—and soon find ourselves in the high, cavernous clockwork laboratory. On one side is Felix Fossil's wall of neatly pegged tools. On the other, standing motionless and surrounded by scaffolding, is the headless body of the metal giant.

And suddenly I'm hit by a burning, *raging,* urge to haul the bronze head over to that body and put it back where it belongs. There's even a winch and crane set up right there, on the scaffolding, ready to go. I could do it! I'm a Lost-and-Founder, after all—this is where the head *should* be!

"Herbie, what are you doing?" Violet gasps, and I find that I am actually pulling the head toward the body, almost making Violet trip as she struggles to keep hold of it. "Herbie!"

"Sorry!' I say, correcting myself, and following Violet's lead again. "I just . . . I just *really . . .*"

"I know you do, Herbie," Violet says, as we reach the door that leads to the hotel elevator and safety. "But we aren't here to repair clockwork robots, no matter how amazing they may be. We're here to stop that crook Eels from getting hold of its brain. Now, *come on!*"

Violet grabs the doorknob above the gargoyle keyhole and turns it.

Nothing happens.

She turns it again, desperately, but to no effect.

"Locked!" Violet cries, putting down the head and kicking the door in exasperation. "Of course it is. Why *wouldn't* it be?"

Behind us, we can hear the sound of whistling. Sebastian Eels, who I imagine has ridden the little train down in triumph, is following at a leisurely pace, knowing we cannot get out.

"There must be some way to open this!" Violet says, leaning against the door. "Herbie, surely there's a tool here we can use."

"Oh dear, oh dear, oh dear," comes the mocking voice of our pursuer, from the other end of the service corridor. "Thank you, both, for doing all the heavy lifting, but now it looks like I'll have to get rid of you, after all. You just can't be trusted."

And we hear the rattle of nails and metal shards as Sebastian Eels starts reloading his blunderbuss.

CHAPTER 35

THE CATCH

Violet moves quickly. Leaving me with the bronze head, she runs back to the laboratory door and slams it shut. There is a large stack of shelves behind it, and without a single thought for the mess she's making, Violet tips the shelves. Everything on them crashes onto the floor, and the shelves jam against the door just in time.

There's a loud crash from the other side of the door, as Eels tries to break in.

"You're only delaying the inevitable," he shouts. There's another crash, and the shelf unit slides a little as Eels starts to force it.

Violet leans against the door.

"Herbie! I can't hold him!"

I clutch my cap in desperation. But then I feel Clermit nestled inside there. He could pick the lock as quick as quick, and I could kick myself for not bringing his key . . .

The key!

I look over at the vast collection of tools on the wall, all neatly arranged by Mrs. Fossil's ancestor . . .

"That's it!" I cry. "There must be winder keys here somewhere."

I start scanning along the display, urgently searching.

There is another bang, louder than ever, and the door comes partly open. Eels gets his arm round and grabs at Violet.

"Herbie!"

And then, I see it. A number 3 square-pin winder key, exactly where it should be. I reach up to where it hangs on its nail.

"Thank you, Felix!" I cry.

But before I can grab the key or do anything else, Eels finally bursts the door open, knocking Violet to the ground.

"I'm tempted to blast one of you now," Eels snarls, aiming his blunderbuss at Violet but turning to glare at me, "just to teach the other one a lesson."

I slip Clermit behind my back out of sight, still unwound. I look up at the key. Can I still get hold of it . . . ?

"Wait!" I say. "You shouldn't blast either of us. Because, if you do . . ." I hunt around my frazzled brain looking for something clever to say. "Er . . ."

"Yes?" says Eels, with a bored expression.

"Because . . ." I blurt, quickly, "because you need us to open the panel on the robot's head to get the gyroscopic regulator out. It won't open unless the head is fixed on the robot's body. There's a . . . a safety catch that seals the panel shut if the robot's head is removed from its shoulders."

Eels lowers his weapon.

"I don't believe you," he growls. But then he adds, "How do you know there's a safety catch?"

I edge over to the workshop table and point at Mr. Ludo's fabulously detailed diagram of the robot, still rolled out there for all to see.

"I saw it on here," I explain with a shrug.

Eels drags Violet to her feet and pushes her toward me.

"Put the head on the desk!" he orders. "I need to see this for myself."

Together, Violet and I heave the bronze head onto the table. Then we back away, hands in the air, allowing Eels to inspect the panel on the top.

"Is that true?" Violet whispers. "About the safety catch?"

"Actually," I whisper back, "I think it is."

"Damn!" Eels cries, scrabbling at the panel with a

screwdriver but still unable to open it. He points the blunder-buss at us again.

"Carry this head up the scaffolding and get it fixed in place. Then *I'll* come up and open the panel. Congratulations. You two have just become useful again."

And so, lifting the bronze head one more time, Violet and I stagger toward the scaffolding.

"There's a winch and crane," I explain, guiding the head toward the contraption I saw earlier. "We'll never get it up there otherwise."

"More lifting," says Sebastian Eels, "and less talking."

We get the head attached to the crane. The antique scaf-folding creaks under this new weight. Then, taking a side each, Violet and I crank the winch that winds the rope, sending a wooden crate, with its precious cargo, up the scaffolding.

"Finally!" Eels grins. "With the regulator in hand, I will have a map—the only map ever made—of the Netherways. I alone will know the way! I alone will find the deepest secret of Eerie-on-Sea."

"What's so important about this 'deepest secret,' anyway?" Violet demands, as we brace the winch and let go of the handles. "If you've never seen it, whatever it is, how do you know it's even there?"

Eels doesn't reply.

"It's probably just money or jewels or something," Violet adds. "Purple Pimm's treasure, perhaps, that you want to get your filthy hands on."

At this, Eels laughs.

"You know, it's almost a shame this robot is no longer functional. It is, uniquely, the only being who has ever seen the deepest secret and returned to tell the tale. At least," he adds, winking at me, "the only one with any memory of it. A memory that is recorded in the gyroscopic regulator of its little clockwork brain."

"Maybe it is functional!" I shout back, annoyed once again by this sense that Eels knows something about my past. "Maybe, when we put the head back on, it'll whir into life and squish you into jellied eel!"

"Ah, you'd like that, wouldn't you, Herbie?" Sebastian Eels chuckles. "And maybe that *is* what will happen. Though after two hundred years moldering down here without even being oiled, something tells me I don't have much to worry about."

"Actually," I start to say, "it seems quite well oiled . . ."

But Violet silences me with a nudge.

"Fix the head in place, Herbert Lemon!" Eels commands. "Unleash your vengeance! Or, as is more likely, unleash the safety catch so that I may claim my prize."

Violet and I glance at each other and shrug. Then I start the lonely climb up the scaffolding, to the summit of the monster, where the head awaits in the swinging crate.

"And remember, Herbie," Eels calls up to me, his blunderbuss braced comfortably in the crook of one arm, its barrels aimed at Violet. "Your friend here is only one very twitchy finger away from oblivion."

As I reach the robot's chest cavity, I slow down. There is that weirdly shaped gap there that I noticed earlier. What is it about this that seems so familiar? Through the gap, I see the wondrous clockwork workings of the metal giant. And within this, in the center of it all, the coil of the enormous steel spring that once provided the robot with its clockwork power. I frown as I notice something I wasn't expecting.

"Wait!" I say, pointing through the gap in the workings. "I've just noticed something I wasn't expecting."

"Get that head fixed," Eels roars. *"I will have my regulator!"*

"Yes, but . . ." I start to say, ". . . if I do that, I think . . ."

Eels swings his weapon up to aim it directly at me.

"OK, OK!" I squeak. "I'm fixing, I'm *fixing!*"

I finally reach the shoulders and the gaping neck of the robot. With an effort, I manage to slide the head off the crate and drag it roughly—though not yet properly—into place. I look down and see that Violet is staring up at me with a look of concern. I give her a discreet nod, which I hope tells her she's right to be concerned. It must do, because she starts to edge away.

"Do it, boy!" Eels shouts. "Quit stalling!"

And what can I do but obey?

I pull at the head, trying to line it up with the neck, when suddenly the metal is tugged from my fingers. There must be magnets, because the head snaps into position, directly above the neck. There are clicks and clunks as control parts and drive shafts snap together and engage. The head settles on the neck and shoulders, seemingly as firmly as the day the robot was first constructed.

"And now," says Sebastian Eels, tossing a screwdriver up to me, "open the head panel. Careful now, boy—the gyroscopic regulator is fragile. Bring it safely down, and I may even let you live."

I catch the screwdriver. But I hesitate.

"What are you waiting for?" Eels calls up.

And that, right there, is the question. What *am* I waiting for? And, more importantly, *why hasn't it happened yet?* I'm just wondering if I've misread the situation completely when I hear something.

We *all* hear something.

From deep inside the broad metal chest of Festergrimm's robot comes a loud *CLUNK*, as if some huge mechanism has just engaged.

And that thing I spotted earlier? Through the gap in the robot's chest? Only that the mighty steel spring is *wound up already*. And whether this was done by Felix Fossil, or someone else, hardly matters now, because—with a ringing clatter of metal plates—the bronze giant starts to vibrate.

And then the roaring starts.

CHAPTER 36

FESTERGRIMM AWAKES

The cavernous laboratory fills with sound. It's the whirring, clamoring, clicking, and ticking sounds you'd get if every clock in the world's biggest clock museum was suddenly overwound and set working at double time. An oily wind rushes up from gaps in the bronze plates as gears grind and flywheels spin, and the great clockwork giant begins to hum with power.

"What have you done?" Eels staggers back in disbelief. "Switch it off!"

"I tried to tell you," I call back, clinging to the scaffolding, which is in danger of being shaken to pieces. I wouldn't be surprised if the antique spring, after all these years being wound and ready, didn't burst out of the robot's chest and kill us all.

But then the frantic vibration subsides, and the great mechanical roar settles down into the steady whirring of a functioning clockwork engine.

The robot's head turns, spinning slowly in a complete circle—once, twice, three times—before returning to the forward position.

From an iron bell inside the mouth grille, there comes, echoing around the cavern a . . .

PANG!

Then, making me cover my ears, a second chime . . .

DONG!

. . . followed by a third . . .

RANG!

"Pandora?" I say, unable to stop myself.

The metal giant turns his head creakingly to look straight at me, where I crouch on its shoulder. The lamp eyes blaze on, flooding me with golden light.

"PAN' DO' RA'?" chime the bells, right into my face.

"Me?" I reply. "N-no, not exactly!"

The light from the lamps turns red.

One of the robot's huge bronze arms—thick as a driftwood tree trunk—begins to rise up, shattering the scaffolding like it's made of matchsticks. On the end of that arm, a giant, three-fingered bronze fist reaches to crush me.

But I'm already falling—tumbling down in a cascade of splintered wood.

"Argh!" is all I manage to say as I disappear under a heap of ruin and planks.

"Herbie!" Violet shouts.

With an ear-splitting creak, the robot leans forward, and his eye lamps spill bloodred light over her.

"PAN' DO' RA?"

"No!" cries Vi. "No, but we can *help* . . ."

A screech of metal drowns out her words as Festergrimm's robot sweeps his fist straight toward her. Violet dives to the ground, rolling as the fist passes through the space where she was just standing, demolishing the second stack of scaffolding with a *boom*. The crane topples forward and smashes across the work desk.

I clamber out of the wreckage and crawl toward Violet. I'm just in time to see Sebastian Eels—cowering by the work desk with a look of bewilderment and terror on his face—raise the blunderbuss at the metal giant and pull the trigger.

There is an almighty explosion.

The weapon spits out fire, kicking back and carrying Eels with a cry up onto the desk. A blast of white-hot metal shot smashes with great force against the robot's torso. The bronze chest plate, hanging loosely open, takes the full force of the blast, and its hinges

shatter. The plate falls with the clang of a temple gong, leaving the robot's whirring clockwork insides exposed for all to see.

Then, just as I think my brain can take no more surprises, Festergrimm's robot starts to grow—his legs and arms elongating as they telescope out with a series of deafening clanking sounds. Now the metal giant can barely fit in the cavern. His back is bent across the ceiling as he looks directly down at Sebastian Eels, pouring the red eye light all over him.

"Get away!" Eels cries, scrabbling onto the desk and desperately pointing his weapon upward. He's pulling the trigger again and again, but he had only reloaded one barrel.

"PAN' DO' RA'!" thunders the robot's mouth bells.

Then he punches one huge metal fist down at Sebastian Eels. I just have time to see Eels start to roll as the desk explodes under the impact, and everything vanishes into a cloud of dust and tools and flying spare parts.

Vi and I stand there for a moment, clutching each other as if we can't quite believe we're both still alive.

The robot, towering over us in the vaulted cavern, swings his fist like a wrecking ball straight into the wall of tools. The whole lot—so neatly arranged by Felix Fossil all those years ago—comes crashing down in a landslide of metalwork. Even if Eels survived the smashing of the desk, he is buried now beneath a drift of tools and wreckage.

But I only have eyes for one tool: the number 3 square-pin winder key I tried to reach earlier. I watch it bounce across the flagstones, and I dive to scoop it up.

"The locked door!" Violet yells above the din, pointing at the one thing stopping us from reaching the hotel elevator and safety. "Maybe the robot can smash it . . ."

Before I can stop her, she runs to it, waving her arms to attract the robot's attention. Which is bonkers, obviously, but very Violet. The robot swings its fist, destroying the metal door like it's made of cardboard. But the tunnel beyond—and with it our hopes of escape—also collapses, in a roar of falling bricks and a great cloud of mortar dust.

"Violet!" I yell as I lose sight of my friend.

"PAN' DO' RA'?" comes the only reply, as the robot rings the name of his maker's long-lost daughter. He creaks back around, turning to find me again with his searchlight eyes.

"Run!" yells Violet, emerging from the dust cloud at high speed. She pulls me toward the other door—the one that leads back the way we came.

We dash into the waxworks workshop and slam the door behind us. There is another *BOOM!* as something else in the laboratory is smashed into ruin.

"What's it doing?" Violet demands, coughing out brick dust. "It's just destroying everything."

"Like in the legend," I reply.

"No, Herbie," says Vi. "*Not* like in the legend. At least, not in the version my dad wrote. But here it seems so full of rage."

"It was made to protect Pandora," I say, as the sounds of destruction grow louder. "It was always a fighting machine."

"But it had to find her, to protect her," Violet replies. "It was a *finding* machine, first and foremost."

There comes a final, calamitous sound, as if the whole laboratory chamber has collapsed. The door we just came through is knocked off its hinges.

"Come on!" I cry, spluttering in this new cloud of brick dust. I pull Violet toward the last remaining exit and whatever safety we can find in the waxworks gallery beyond.

"Wait . . ." Violet says. "Look!"

Back where the laboratory was, as the clouds swirl, we see one huge metal leg suspended bizarrely in the air. Then it rises up, vanishing through the ceiling. We dare to creep nearer, blinking in the dust, and finally understand what we're seeing. The clockwork giant—Festergrimm's terrifying robot—has broken through the roof of the laboratory and is climbing up through the hole.

And out into Eerie-on-Sea.

CHAPTER 37

COGZILLA!

Vi and I clamber back into the ruined laboratory, over bricks and tools, and look up. Above us—through the swirl of brick dust—we see a huge round hole. And high above that, in the night sky—as if startled to be visible to us at all—winks a single star.

Then we hear the screaming.

"We've got to stop it!" Violet says.

"Er," I reply, *"how?"*

"Come on, Herbie!" is the only answer I get, as Violet begins to climb the pile of debris.

So, I come on—grabbing and heaving and somehow

managing to climb up after Violet until we pull ourselves out of the hole made by the bronze robot, and stand panting on the cobblestones of Fargazi Round. Behind us, swathed in clouds of brick dust, is Festergrimm's Eerie Waxworks. Lights are coming on all around the square as people step into the street, or lean out of upstairs windows, to see what could be making such a terrible noise. And what they see makes their eyes go wide.

Up ahead, in Gazbaleen Alley, is a trail of destruction. Several houses have lost their fronts completely, and fires are starting. People are running to throw buckets of water, while others are lying dazed in the street in their pajamas, wondering what has happened. One man is sitting in his bath, even though his bath is now in the middle of the road and full of plaster and brick. And beyond all this, just visible above the rooftops, the robot's bronze head gleams in the smoky moonlight as the it advances through the streets, its angry red eye lights turning here and there like a lighthouse gone mad.

Searching.

"PAN' DO' RA'?" chime the great iron bells in the machine's mouth.

Then is another crash as the giant demolishes a chimney stack.

We start to run after the robot, as people yell and dash here and there in panic. Already we see some pulling out makeshift weapons—walking sticks, axes, and in one case a cricket bat—shouting to others to do the same.

"Wait, Herbie," Violet calls, skidding to a halt at the top of Dieppe Steps. "Look, he's turning toward the sea. Let's head him off."

Sure enough, judging by the beams of red light in the clouds of dust and smoke, the metal giant has begun moving toward the promenade.

We run into Tenby Twist, coming to a halt at the bottom of the stone steps there, as more Eerie folk emerge from their houses to discover what disaster is befalling them.

"What's happening?" voices demand.

"Festergrimm!" comes an answering cry. "Like in the old tales!"

"It's true!" A young boy leans out of a window high above and points. "I can see him! He's coming!"

Panic begins to set in, but Vi and I hold our ground, looking back up the steps.

Where the bronze giant has just appeared.

He's a terrible sight—towering as big as a house, with his legs and arms telescoped out. He swings his fists, smashing windows and taking out chunks of wall, as his head turns this way and that.

"PAN' DO' RA'?"

"Why is he smashing things, Herbie?" Violet asks. "There must be a reason."

"He can't find Pandora," I reply.

"But he was *built* to find her," Violet says. "He's even calling her name. It's like he doesn't even know what that name means anymore. Is he . . . is he faulty in some way? After all these years?"

I shrug. Maybe, if I'd had more time with the plans in the laboratory before they were destroyed, I'd be able to answer that.

"There was something in your dad's book about the robot being damaged," I say, suddenly remembering. "About a part falling off . . ."

Violet blinks at me.

"Of course!" she cries, grabbing me by both shoulders.

Then she turns me back toward the metal giant, who is standing tower-tall at the top of the steps, as if undecided where to go next. By now, bricks thrown by the angry townsfolk are bouncing feebly off his metal plating.

"Hey!" Violet yells, at the top of her lungs. "Hey, Festergrimm! Over here! Pandora! PAN-DO-RA!"

The bronze giant, hearing her through mechanical ears I can barely imagine, turns his head toward us with an echoing creak. The light from his eye lamps changes from red to golden as they shine down the steps and onto us.

"PAN' DO' RA'?" chime the bells.

"That's right! Pandora!" Violet shouts in reply, waving her arms. "This way!"

Festergrimm lifts one bronze foot and starts crashing down the stairs toward us.

"Violet!" I clutch my cap. "What have you done?"

But Violet ignores me as she waves her arms again to draw the robot ever closer.

"You do know there are no soldiers in the castle these days, right?" I gasp. "And no navy warships to save us. Violet, *what are you doing?*"

"Herbie!" Violet cries, pointing at the approaching robot. "In my dad's book, the robot didn't start attacking the town until *after* it was damaged. Something *did* fall out of his chest."

"Well, yes . . . but how can we know what that was?"

"Can't you guess?" Vi replies. And she points at my Lost-and-Founder's cap.

And now, finally, with a zap like a bolt of lightning, I get why the funny-shaped gap in the chest of the robot has been causing me such a brain niggle.

I snatch off my cap and tip Clermit into my hand.

I gawp at the shell in amazement.

He's not just one of Mr. Ludo's long-lost clockwork toys, as I've suspected since I saw him laid out on Dr. Thalassi's desk.

"Clermit," I cry, "is *part* of the robot!"

"That's why Eels wanted him back," Violet says. "And he's not just any part . . ."

I think of the little crystal lozenge within Clermit, with the fine golden wire inside. I remember what the doc said about the great source of power that would be needed to give purpose to a clockwork giant.

"It's not a golden wire," I whisper in wonder. "It's a hair! In the crystal—a single golden hair from Pandora's head. Festergrimm doesn't just have a clockwork brain. He also has a heart!"

"Except," says Violet, pulling me out of this moment of wonder and back into the very dangerous present, "right now, he *doesn't!*"

With a tremendous crash, the metal giant reaches the bottom of the stairs, smashing the front of yet another house. He vanishes from view in a cloud of dust and smoke, until only his blazing red eyes remain, fixed relentlessly on us.

"Without his heart," Violet gasps as we back away, "Festergrimm has no purpose at all. He's as lost as Pandora herself."

Festergrimm towers over Tenby Twist now and the roof of the Whelk & Walrus Pub, and from his mouth his ringing bells batter our ears with their tragic question.

"PAN' DO' RA'?"

And so, we run. Onto the promenade and along the seafront, we run as fast as we can.

"But how do we get *this*," I gasp, waggling Clermit in my hand, "up *there*?"

And I point back at the robot's chest cavity and the shell-shaped gap in his workings.

Festergrimm steps out onto the promenade, shattering the cobblestones under his enormous weight as he finds us again with his spotlight eyes.

"We need . . . to get up high," Vi says between breaths. "Where can we climb, Herbie?"

"The hotel . . ." I manage to say. "The fire escape . . ."

"Then come on!" Violet says, turning back to the robot, waving her arms. "Over here! PANDORA! Over here!"

And the robot, who bears his creator's name—the creaking of his mighty limbs mixing with the waves crashing in Eerie Bay—strides toward us in pursuit.

CHAPTER 38

FIRE ESCAPE

A s we run toward the Grand Nautilus Hotel, yet more people are leaning out of windows or coming fearfully into the street. No one seems to notice Vi and me— all eyes are on the bronze colossus towering in the smoky air behind, striding after us on telescoped legs, eye lamps ablaze.

But since each step for Festergrimm is about twenty steps for a Herbie or a Violet, he's gaining on us, and *fast*!

"This way!" Violet shouts, still waving. Then we duck into a side alley, toward the rickety hotel fire escape. We start rattling up it. The third story should be high enough to reach the bronze giant's chest.

"Ah, Herbie," says a voice, and a head emerges from a hotel

window just above me. It's Colonel Crabwise. "I might have known you'd have the situation under control. Good lad!"

As I blink in surprise to see him there, Mrs. Crabwise puts her head out, too.

"Are you returning a lost thing?" she says. "I do love to see a little lost-and-foundering in action."

"I am!" I gasp in reply, touching my cap with a little salute. "This!"

And I hold up the gleaming, pearlescent shell of my clock-work hermit crab.

With a vast metallic creak, Festergrimm reaches the alley-way and turns to shine his eye lamps right at me. He gives off another angry peal from his mouth bells as he pushes into the alleyway toward us, sending cracks up the side of the Grand Nautilus Hotel.

"Bladderwracks!" I gasp.

And that's when another window opens, right beside me, and an annoying head pops out.

"What the blazes is going on?" says Mr. Mollusc. Then, when he sees me there, he adds, like it's all my fault, "You! I might have known."

"One more flight, Herbie," Violet cries, pulling me up the steps to the third floor of the fire escape. "There! We can reach from here."

"Do you think . . . ?" I start to say, clutching the wall and watching the great bronze head advancing toward us. "Do you think I should wind up Clermit now?"

"What?" Violet turns her disbelieving eyes to me. "You mean you *haven't*? Yes!"

I brace myself against the fire escape and fish the winder key from my pocket. I'm just about to put it into the hole in Clermit's shell and give him three good windings-up as I always do, when there's a deafening crack right beside us. The fire escape shifts under our feet as Festergrimm—pushing ever deeper into the narrow alley—smashes one end of the metal staircase clean off the wall.

Our section of fire escape swings out into the alleyway, carrying us with it.

"Whaa . . . ?" I say as I fall against the handrail, the shell knocked from my hand. I manage to stop Clermit from rolling off the steps with my shoe, but the key flies out. It falls to the flight of stairs below and skitters across the topmost metal step, far beyond our reach. Now I'm left clinging on for all my buttons are worth, one leg out like a rubbish ballerina, my toe the only thing stopping Clermit from falling to the street below.

"Herbie!" Violet calls from where she also clings. But if I think Vi's shouting out of concern for her favorite Lost-and-Founder, I soon see that she isn't. She is pointing in disbelief at

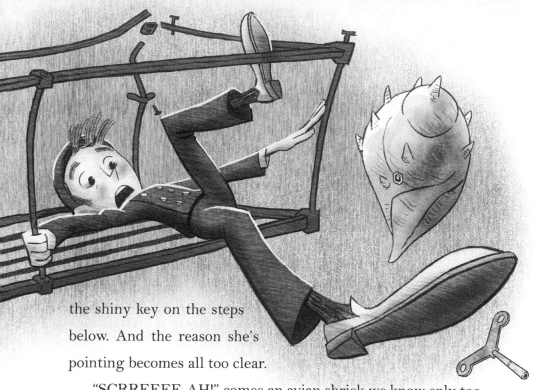

the shiny key on the steps below. And the reason she's pointing becomes all too clear.

"SCRREEEE-AH!" comes an avian shriek we know only too well, and a seagull lands beside the key. The scrap of blue plastic bag on his leg is flapping in the wind.

"Bagfoot!"

The seagull tips his head at us one way, and then the other. Then he looks down at the key and gives it a peck.

"Here, boy!" Violet calls, leaning out from the fire escape, making enticing seagull-ish noises. "That's it. Bring it, there's a good gull."

The seagull pecks again, nudging the key nearer the edge of the step.

By now the robot has moved on, losing interest in us and

pounding farther up the alley. Our chance to reach the giant's chest—the reason we climbed up here in the first place—is slipping away.

"Come *on*, Bagfoot!" Violet pleads. "You owe me, you pesky bird. Bring us the key!"

Now, Violet Parma has a way with animals. Even animals that most people don't like. Even some animals most people think don't *exist*. She is what they call an "animal lover." So, if anyone in the world can persuade a scruffy old seagull to lend a helping beak to save our town from being flattened by an out-of-control clockwork juggernaut with fists like wrecking balls, it's Violet. Even so, I'm still amazed when Bagfoot—with a final tip of his scraggly head at Vi—pecks down at the key and . . .

Picks it up!

"Yes!" Violet cries, beckoning madly. "That's it! Oh, you beautiful herring gull, you!"

But Bagfoot, as we can now see, isn't alone. His band of buddies, seeing their famous blue-footed captain seemingly peck up some tasty morsel, swoop in for their share. In a moment there is pandemonium on the steps below us, as half a dozen seagulls fight in a mad flap of white wings and angry shrieks.

And the key? Well, that gets dropped, of course.

It clatters down the stairs and onto the cobblestones in the alley, three stories below.

"No!" Violet shouts.

"Now what do we do?" I demand, looking madly at Festergrimm's vast bronze back as he advances away from the hotel. I've got Clermit safely back in my hands, but I can't reach the robot's chest anymore. And we can't get to the rest of the fire escape either, not to go up or down, because the bit we're on is swinging crazily out from the hotel wall.

By now, a ragtag group of fisherfolk from the harbor have reached the robot and are jabbing at it with long boat hooks and harpoons. More appear at the top of Dieppe Steps, scaling the walls with a fishing net between them.

"Maybe the fisherfolk can deal with it," I say, not feeling hopeful.

"They'll get themselves killed," Violet replies as the metal giant stamps at the fisherfolk, causing them to scatter. "Hold on, Herbie—we're going to have to lean together."

And Violet lets herself fall hard out from the handrail, till she's leaning crazily into the void. Closing my eyes and muttering "bladderwracks!" for all I'm worth, I do the same, and this shifts the weight of the loose section of fire escape, swinging it back to its original position. Then Violet jumps.

"Ah, acrobatics!" says the colonel to Mrs. Crabwise. "Jolly good. I always did like dinner and a show."

Violet lands with a clang on the metal steps below and starts running down the stairs to the street.

"Call to him, Herbie!" she cries. "Call Festergrimm back!"

My mind boggles at this. The robot, which I've been dreaming about in all its clockwork wonder since I first heard of it, holds rather less fascination for me now that he's running amok and destroying my home. And Violet wants me to call him *back*?

"UM . . ." I shout at the top of my voice. "ER . . . YOO-HOO? OVER HERE?"

It doesn't sound very convincing, even to me. To be honest, any command that ends with a question mark is a bit floppy. For a moment I consider adding a *please* on the end, but that would probably make it worse. Then I find myself shouting another word, as loud as I possibly can.

"PANDORA!" I yell. "PAN! DOR! RA!"

The bronze giant gives out a great creak of joints and ceases his attempts to crush the fisherfolk of Eerie-on-Sea. Like a searchlight seeking out a target, his metal head turns one hundred eighty degrees, until his eye lamps find me again, where I am clinging to the wobbly metal stairs clutching Clermit.

"PAN' DO' RA'?" chime the mouth bells in jubilant hope.

Then, his eyes remaining fixed on me, the robot's body turns one hundred eighty, too, in a crescendo of metallic shrieks.

"Vi!" I squeak. "It's working, but . . . now what?"

Violet has reached the cobblestones and is running down the alley toward the knot of squabbling gulls. She pulls out the stale croissant she pocketed earlier.

"Hey!" she shouts at Bagfoot and his shrieking bandits. "Fancy a snack?" And she tosses the croissant high into the air. Instantly, the seagulls flap up after it, pecking each other out of the way, snatching and snipping and *tearing* the pastry apart midflight.

While Violet dives for the winder key.

"Got it!" she shouts, holding it up.

"Great!" I reply. I'm still clutching Clermit in my hands, one arm looped around the handrail, as Festergrimm comes to a halt right before me. I can see his mighty workings whirring and driving with great force deep inside his chest, while his golden eye light nearly blinds me.

"Hello!" I say.

The eye light shifts instantly back to angry red.

Festergrimm lifts his great bronze hand up to seize and crush the one who promised Pandora but can't deliver.

Me!

"Herbie!" Violet shouts. "Herbie, *catch*!"

And she throws up the winder key as hard as she can.

CHAPTER 39

THE HEART OF THE MATTER

I've never been much of one for catching. Catching is not on the list of things a Lost-and-Founder needs to be good at. But as the brass key sails up toward me, I realize that this is something I should probably catch the first time.

Which is why it's really annoying when I don't.

But, before you shout at me—before you join Vi in rolling your eyes as the shiny key flies past my hand—I should explain. I *would* have caught the key—I just *know* I would have—if at that exact moment I hadn't seen something unexpected appear just behind Violet. Or rather, some*one*.

Someone haggard and battered, with hair all crazy and clothes torn and bloody.

Someone with a look of rage on his bruised face and an antique blunderbuss in his hands.

"And that's for *you!*" snarls Sebastian Eels, thumping Violet hard in the back with the butt of his weapon, knocking her to the ground.

Then he whirls a rope lasso—once, twice—and on the third whirl releases it. The lasso flies up and drops neatly around the robot's neck.

Just as the robot's enormous, grasping hand reaches me.

And so, I drop. It's all I can think to do. I drop to the metal steps of the wobbly fire escape as the great bronze hand smashes the handrail, right where I was just standing. I barely have time to roll aside as he bangs his fist down at me like a hammer. The already-battered section of fire escape shudders with the impact and starts to give way completely.

I look down.

I can't see Violet, but I *can* see Sebastian Eels—the blunderbuss on a strap over his shoulder—pulling himself up the rope toward Festergrimm's head. And he's halfway there already!

"Vi!" I shout down to the alley, but there's no reply.

The fire escape gives a final, sickening creak.

"Violet," I yell, *"look out!"*

And then I do the only thing I can think of in the

circumstances: I shove Clermit back under my cap and leap off the collapsing metal steps . . .

. . . and grab hold of the robot itself!

I cling desperately to one of Festergrimm's enormous armor plates, as the fire escape finally breaks away from the wall of the hotel and crashes down to the street below.

"Nice try!" shouts Sebastian Eels up at me, as he swings to avoid the falling stairs.

Now I'm dangling high above street level, just below the robot's open chest. The roofs of Eerie-on-Sea are spread around me, wreathed in smoke, and the yells of the town's distress. The fisherfolk have rallied and are approaching the robot from two sides, armed to the teeth. If anyone in Eerie-on-Sea can stop the great bronze machine, it is probably these hardy people (though my money would still be on the robot).

And then I see the key. Gleaming in the moonlight, on a higher section of fire escape still attached to the wall. I'm just thinking I'll have to climb up the robot itself to reach it when something happens to answer the problem for me. With a great creak, Festergrimm raises one foot, smashes it firmly through a ground-floor window, and begins to climb.

The clockwork giant is *climbing the Grand Nautilus Hotel*!

With me still clinging on to his front like a startled limpet.

As the robot climbs, I dart out one hand and grab the winder key. Above, I see the flock of seagulls—their croissant finished—swooping and diving at the machine, hunting for crumbs. The metal giant turns his head lamps this way and that as if confused by the birds, but his climb continues.

Why is he climbing?

Suddenly I understand. Sebastian Eels has reached the robot's head. I imagine that even now he is working at the little hatch that contains the gyroscopic regulator, trying to force it open to grab the prize inside. The robot, in its simple mechanical understanding of the situation, is climbing to try to reach the unwelcome passenger.

Meanwhile, the other unexpected passenger—me!—needs to get his arm around something firm, so he can free his hands to wind up Clermit and get him home. The shell-shaped gap in the robot's chest is just above me now.

"I promised I'd get you home," I say to Clermit, "and that's exactly what I'll do."

I reach up and grab a metal rod in the robot's chest. The inner workings of the clockwork giant spin and judder and whir with a furious speed, pumping out a metallic wind of hot air. The rod I'm holding is almost too hot to touch, but I slip my arm around it. Festergrimm is still climbing, but my hands are free.

"What is the meaning of this?" demands a crackly old voice I'm not expecting to hear but should be.

The robot has reached the roof. Lady Kraken—tucked up in her bronze-and-wicker wheelchair—trundles toward us over her rooftop balcony. She has the habitual silken turban on her head, and the box of Turkish delight is in her lap. Her eyes are rounder than I've ever seen them.

"Herbert Lemon?" she says, seeing me clinging there. "I hope you aren't the cause of all this hullabaloo."

"Not exactly, Your Ladyness," I manage to reply through gasps of effort. I pull Clermit back out from beneath my cap. "It's just a little Lost-and-Founder business, got out of hand. I'll have it sorted in a sec."

"It's not Herbie's fault," says another voice, and I'm amazed and relieved to see Violet running out onto the balcony. She must have gotten back into the hotel and run up the inside stairs to reach Lady Kraken's private chambers.

"Violet!" Lady Kraken beams with pleasure.

"It's him!" cries Vi, pointing up at the robot's head. "Lady Kraken, it's all Sebastian Eels's fault!"

Eels has a screwdriver and is using it to prize open the little panel at last, a look of triumph on his face. The robot himself, seemingly confused about how to stop what is happening on his own head, is sweeping one free arm at the still-circling seagulls.

"I might have known!" Lady Kraken narrows her eyes again to two turtle slits of anger as she spies Eels up there. "Get this confounded contraption off my hotel this instant. Then pack your bags, Sebastian Eels, and never darken the streets of Eerie-on-Sea again."

"Lady Kraken," Eels starts to say from the shoulders of the robot. "I can explain . . ."

But then he must realize there's nothing he can say to hide his villainy now, so instead he curls his lip.

"Oh, to hell with it!" he snaps. "Why don't you shut your mouth, you rangy old bat? I don't need you or your moldy wax-works now, anyway."

Lady Kraken, who has probably never been spoken to in this way for all her hundred and something years, clenches her fists with a crinkle of twiggy joints.

"Herbert Lemon!" she cries, pointing. "Stop that crazy author!"

"Just doing it, Lady K!" I reply, slipping the winder key into Clermit's shell. "One stopped author coming up."

"Oh, no you don't!" Eels yells, leaning outward to point his blunderbuss down at me.

"Oh, bladderwracks!" I yell, flattening myself against the robot's armored plating.

I'm fairly sure the gun won't blast me if I stay flat. But I can't do a thing while I'm stuck like this.

"One move from you, boy," Eels shouts down, leaning even farther to find a new line of sight, "and I'll repaint the hotel a lovely shade of blasted Lemon."

"I won't let you!" Violet shouts at Eels.

"Yeah?" says Eels, as he finally gets a good angle on me and squints down the barrel of the blunderbuss. "You and whose army?"

"I don't have an army . . ." Violet replies.

"Exactly!" Eels starts to squeeze the trigger.

"I have an air force!"

And with this Violet grabs the box of Turkish delight from Lady Kraken's lap and flings it up at Sebastian Eels like a Frisbee.

It hits him on the head.

The lid pops off in a puff of icing sugar, and Turkish delight rains down over him—sticking in his hair and getting caught in his clothes.

"A hit!" cries Lady Kraken. "And right on the noggin, too."

Eels yells in fury, spluttering and wiping at his eyes.

"What the . . . ?" he shouts, picking bits of candy off himself. "Why, you little . . ."

But that's all he says. Because right then Bagfoot, with his ravenous squadron of Eerie-on-Seagulls, dives for the attack.

CHAPTER 40

"DEATH TO FESTERGRIMM!"

Sebastian Eels is engulfed in wings and shrieking. He swipes uselessly with his blunderbuss, until—pointing it in desperation at the first seagull he can distinguish—he pulls the trigger.

There is an explosion of light and a *BOOM!* like a cannon, and even the scrap of blue plastic bag on the seagull's leg vanishes from view in the roar of flame and red-hot nails.

"Bagfoot!" Violet and I shout together.

It's funny how you only discover you'll miss someone—even someone as annoying as Violet's rescued seagull—when they are being blasted to atoms by a desperate author on top of a giant clockwork robot. But in that instant, as I see Eerie-on-Sea's foremost chips-and-doughnut thief getting thoroughly blasted to smithereens, I can't help feeling that the poor feather-brained nuisance didn't deserve this.

Then the smoke clears, and we see . . .

A seagull, spinning in space, bloodied and singed, with feathers in disarray, but whole! Impossibly, *miraculously* whole! Even though we can hear a hard rain of metal bits from the blunderbuss hammering down across the rooftops around us. But then, that's the thing with Eerie-on-Seagulls: nothing can stop them once they've got their beady eyes on your snack.

Bagfoot, flapping his smoldering wings, gives an almighty shriek of indignation and dives onto Eels's head, claws and beak first.

As for Eels, he can do nothing but raise his hands to protect his face. But as he does, he loses his grip on the robot's head and falls off.

"AAARGH!" he cries as he drops to the cobblestones far below, pursued by seagulls.

Leaving me to finally get my hand on the key and give Clermit three good windings-up.

Tic-tic-tic-TIK, Tic-tic-tic-TIK, Tic-tic-tic-TIK

Festergrimm is moving again, turning his head now that the distractions of Eels and the seagulls are gone, looking for something new to smash. His eye lamps find Violet and Lady K on the balcony, and flood them with bloodred light. With a creak of doom, he begins to reach one great bronze hand to crush them.

"Herbie!" Vi cries, clinging on to Lady K's wheelchair.

And *that's* when I, Herbert Lemon—Lost-and-Founder at the Grand Nautilus Hotel—reach up to the gap in the robot's chest where his heart should be and slam Clermit home.

With a *SCHLAAK*, bronze rods slide out to meet him, and his own brass limbs fold out to grasp them. From inside his shell come three bright music-box notes . . .

Pan' Do' Ra'

. . . and all at once Festergrimm judders to a creaking halt, his great crushing hand freezing just over the balcony—and the old lady and the girl who huddle there.

The clockwork roar of the metal giant's inner workings quiets to almost a whisper, and his eye lamps wink out.

There is a moment of eerie silence, marked only by the distant shouts from the townsfolk far below and the crash of the rolling sea. Oh, and also a steady ticking from somewhere deep inside the robot.

Tick

Tick

Tick . . .

And then . . .

TOCK!

With a flurry of clockwork, the inner workings spring back to life, though now they are more measured and less clamorous than before. The robot's eyes glow with a steady new light—warm and golden—and from his mouth chimes a triumphant peal of bells: "PAN' DO' RA'!"

Then, as if none of us are even there—as if nothing else in the world matters at all—the robot begins to climb down from the roof, ringing the name of the long-lost girl.

"Wait for me!" shouts Violet, leaping over the balcony railing and landing on the clockwork giant's shoulders.

"Ah!" cries Lady Kraken, flapping her twiggy hands together with glee as she watches Violet go. "Ah, I wish . . . how I wish . . ."

But what she wishes we do not hear, as the robot drops rapidly down the side of the hotel, his arms and legs moving like, well, like clockwork. I climb up the bronze armor plates to join Violet on the other side of the robot's head.

"Bravo, Herbie!" come the voices of the colonel and Mrs. Crabwise, waving from one window. "Bravo!"

"Lemon!" splutters Mr. Mollusc, leaning out of the shattered remains of another, his mustache full of brick dust. "Just you wait . . ."

But already we are past them, and the robot is back with a clang on the cobblestones. I look around at the smoking ruins of the houses. For a moment, in the chaos of it all, I think I see

Sebastian Eels, sitting on a heap of bricks, untangling his lasso rope from around one ankle, but when I try to get a better look, he's already lost in shadow.

The robot, having reached the street, turns a precise ninety degrees, to face directly up toward Dieppe Steps.

A band of fisherfolk are waiting, heavily armed with vicious weapons and backed up by townspeople. Seemingly oblivious to the threat, Festergrimm takes one creaking step toward this makeshift army, and then another.

"Where are we going?" I ask Violet.

"I don't know," she replies, "but the robot seems to, now that he's got a heart once more. That golden hair in Clermit gives him back his original purpose: to find lost Pandora."

"PAN' DO' RA'!" chimes the metal man, as if in confirmation.

"But," I say, pointing toward the mob, "how is he going to find anything if that lot stops him?"

"It's OK!" Violet yells to the waiting men. "He's not fighting anymore. The battle's over!"

And it's true. Festergrimm is now walking with precise movements, carefully avoiding the buildings. But just in case this hasn't been noticed, and to back up Vi, I take off my Lost-and-Founder's cap and wave it as high as I can, for all to see.

"It's Herbie!" yells a voice from below.

"Aye," shouts a nearby fisherman, "and his friend, Violet!"

"They've been kidnapped!" shouts another voice. "Kidnapped by the monster!"

"No!" Violet waves urgently. "No, you don't understand . . ."

"Death!" roars a particularly burly fisherman, armed with huge metal spike. "Death to Festergrimm!"

"Death!" cry all the fisherfolk and fighters, and they pour down Dieppe Steps, waving their boat hooks and spears. Rocks and bricks start bouncing off the robot, and all around fisherfolk of Eerie start scaling the buildings again, carrying ropes and nets.

"Stop!" Violet shouts, as we cling on tighter. "It's not what you think!"

Through all this, the robot plows ahead, his great clanking strides scattering the people below.

"Fall back!" cries the big fisherman with the metal spike. The spike is bent.

"Bring dynamite!" calls another.

"What?" I cry. "No, *don't* bring dynamite!"

But the defenders of Eerie-on-Sea are regrouping deeper in the town, as some fisherfolk run to their net sheds to gather whatever dangerous things they keep hidden there.

"Where are we going?" says Vi, as Festergrimm turns another crisp ninety degrees and faces up a flight of stone steps, toward Fargazi Round and the waxworks gallery.

"I think . . ." I say, "I think the robot is going to do what it was made to do."

"You don't mean . . . ?"

"I do," I gasp. "I think he is going to continue his search for Pandora."

"But, Herbie"—Violet's eyes go wide as scallops—"that means he's heading for . . ."

"The Netherways." I nod. "And if we don't get off him, we're going, too!"

CHAPTER 41

A HOLE IN THE GROUND

The robot climbs the stairs, turning his chest side-on so that he can glide through the narrow space between the buildings without causing any damage. A few people yell at him from upstairs windows, and a saucepan flies out of one, bouncing off his head and down into the street with a clatter.

"They hate him," says Violet in despair. "Poor robot!"

"For them, he's just the Festergrimm from the legend," I reply as we ride down the street on the giant's shoulders. "That means they expect him to attack the town and, well, *he has*, hasn't he? They don't know any better."

By now the robot has emerged once again into Fargazi

Round. I look down at the waxworks gallery below us and the great crater beside it.

The robot, with his telescopic legs, strides straight over the ruin of the laboratory and makes for an unassuming drain cover set in the road. He comes to a halt before it and begins to shorten his limbs back into themselves, shedding height in a series of creaks and clacks. Soon he is only twice the height of a normal man. He directs his eye lights onto the drain.

"Time to go," says Vi, preparing to jump off.

"Wait . . ." I reply, clinging on to one ear handle of Festergrimm's head. Violet is right, of course, but suddenly my mind is full of . . . something else: full of the crazy notion of *not* jumping off at all, of riding instead with this lost-and-foundering robot forever.

Of helping it find Pandora at long, long last.

"Herbie?" Violet shakes me.

"I think . . ." I start to say. "I . . . I *think* . . ."

But I don't get to say what I think. Without warning, the robot reaches down, grabs the grate in one great fist, and wrenches the whole thing out from the ground, bringing a large section of road with it. Then, with a precise spin of his lower arm, the robot tosses the grate aside, sending it skidding across the square with a spray of sparks.

"We need to get off!" Violet says as we look down into what

is now a gaping hole. Already the robot is stepping into it, reaching one bronze foot down into the dark. "Now!"

"I can't," I say, clinging to the ear handle with both hands now. "I think I'm supposed to go, too, Vi. With the robot. Pandora—she's been lost for so long . . ."

"What?" Violet looks aghast. The implication of my words— a voyage into the dark unknown of the deadly labyrinth beneath Eerie-on-Sea; deep, deep into a secret world of shadow from which no one living has ever returned—is written in Violet's eyes. And when the bravest person you know looks this alarmed . . .

"H-Herbie," Violet stammers, "maybe Nope-vember isn't *always* such a bad idea."

By now Festergrimm has turned and inserted his second leg into the hole. With a series of ratcheting clanks, he starts to lower the rest of himself down.

"You don't have to come," I gasp, even though I'm terrified at the prospect of going alone. "I know it's bonkers, Vi."

"I can't let you do this alone, Herbie," Violet declares, seizing hold of her ear handle with both hands, too, and closing her eyes tight. "I could never do that."

The robot lowers himself farther, till only his head, shoulders, and chest—and the whirring clockwork within—remain above street level. We are moments away from descending into the eternal dark of the Netherways.

But then we hear a voice.

"There it is!" comes a shout. "The metal monster that smashed your homes is trying to escape!"

Sebastian Eels, clutching his blunderbuss in one hand and the familiar trident in the other, is striding across the square toward us. Behind him marches the army of battered fisherfolk, swinging clubs and sticks, determined to defend their town to the end. One fisherman is rolling a barrel with a skull and crossbones painted on the side. That'll be the dynamite, I expect.

"Death to Festergrimm!" calls one of them, as they surround us.

"But rescue those two first!" cries another, pointing his ax at us and adding, "I guess."

"Aye," shouts a third, taking a stick of dynamite from the barrel, "but *then* there's blasting to be done!"

The fisherfolk army roars in approval.

Sebastian Eels steps ahead of all the rest, raising his trident for silence. Even the robot stops, his eye lamps bathing everyone in gold as he pauses in his descent.

"Never fear, dear Herbie and Violet," declares Sebastian Eels, in a dramatic voice, "I'll save you!"

And with this, he rushes forward and plants the barrel of his blunderbuss right into the center of the robot's chest cavity.

"No!" I shout, but it's already too late.

Eels smirks at us as he pulls the trigger.

The explosion rings like a bell inside Festergrimm's bronze chest. The robot shudders, as gouts of fire emerge between his armor plates, then he sags, as his mighty arms—the only thing holding us up above the hole—start to lose power.

Violet and I cling on by reflex, tighter than ever, and can only watch in horror as Eels jumps up the front of the robot. He hammers open the much-battered panel on the robot's head with the middle prong of his trident, and then snatches out what he finds inside.

"Ha!" he cries. "At last!"

There, in his raised hand, is a little silver mouse, its wheels spinning helplessly. It's Mr. Ludo's clockwork Mousie from the legend in Peter Parma's book—the one that can solve any maze. Eels snaps back the mouse's head and reveals a glass lozenge inside, like the one in Clermit that holds the golden hair. But this crystal is filled with the brassy sparkle of tiny, spinning parts.

"The gyroscopic regulator!" I cry.

"And the only map of the Netherways ever made," Eels replies in a whisper only we can hear. "Good luck finding your way without it!"

"No!" Violet shouts, reaching to grab the mouse.

"Yes!" cries Eels, jumping back to the ground and then firing the second barrel of the blunderbuss into the robot's already-damaged workings. The robot shudders again and his strength finally gives out, just as I'm starting a desperate jump for safety. His arms fly up, and he slips into the hole—with Violet still clinging to one ear handle!

And me? Well, I'm falling free, aren't I?

Through the hole.

Tumbling down through empty space into the swallowing dark beneath Eerie-on-Sea.

CHAPTER 42

LOST

··

Time seems to stretch out.

Have you ever had that happen? When time seems to stretch out?

Sometimes I'm the right-way up, and I can see a patch of fire and moonlight above me, shrinking fast as we plummet. And other times I'm the wrong-side down, but I can just about see Violet, clinging on to the robot's head as it falls like a giant green stone beneath me.

A lot of the time I'm in between and can see nothing at all.

But then, suddenly—just as I'm thinking time has stretched almost to a breaking point—there is an almighty clang of metal against rock.

The robot stops falling, and I crash onto his shoulder, bounce off, and start falling again . . .

"Got you!" cries Violet, who—with lightning reflexes—has grabbed me by the sleeve.

"Ooof!" I reply, as I swing hard against the back of the robot and get the wind knocked out of me.

With a few desperate scrabbles, I clamber back onto the robot's shoulder. In the flickering, failing light of the metal giant's eye lamps, my own eyes find Violet's and we stare at each other in shock.

"Wughlg . . ." I manage to say. "Wh-what happened?"

"Well, we aren't dead," Vi gasps. "Or . . . or are we?"

I look up at the robot's arms, which are raised and telescoped out full, and see that Festergrimm's hands have caught onto a ledge above us. He is holding on only by the tips of six bronze fingers and two bronze thumbs.

"That must be the ledge Pandora fell onto," I say, "in the legend."

Beyond this, the patch of light and life above us—the view back up through the hole to the surface—is horribly far away. And below us, if the echoing of the clockwork workings and the buffet of strange subterranean winds is anything to go by, is nothing at all.

"How deep do you think it goes?" Violet asks.

"I'm trying *not* to think about that!" I squeak.

The robot, with a series of loud clicks and clanks, engages his gears and begins to retract his arms, raising us up toward the ledge. But there is an almighty *BANG!* from inside Festergrimm's chest, and the action fails. With a sickening lurch, one of his hands slips off the ledge, causing a rush of shattered rock and stones to rain down around us, *ping-pang*ing off the bronze machine as they fall. Now the robot swings by a single hand, his other arm hanging limp, and we are left clinging desperately to his head.

"Quick, Herbie!" Violet shouts. "Climb!"

Putting our feet into gaps in the metal plates, we clamber up the robot's remaining good arm and pull ourselves onto the rocky ledge.

"Come on!" I cry, leaning urgently back over the edge and reaching down to Festergrimm. "You can do it. Please don't give up!"

The robot looks up at me, the golden light in his eyes dimming.

He starts to retract his remaining arm again, and amazingly—with a grinding of gears—he gets his elbow onto the ledge. If only his other arm would work, he could do this! But then there is another sickening *CLANG!* from the workings in his chest as something else gives way. Cogs and broken parts spill out through a gap in his plating and tumble into the dark below.

"I'm so sorry," I say to the metal man, whose face is just below us now. My eyes are filling with watery sting. "I can't help you!"

There's only one way this is going to end. The damage Eels did with the blunderbuss is just too great. The hatch on top of the giant's head is still open, where Eels snatched the little clockwork mouse containing the regulator. And then, inside the place where the mouse was—lit by the glow of dying eye light—I catch a glimpse of something else deep inside.

"Herbie!" Violet gasps, seeing it, too.

"So," I reply in a horrified whisper, "it's true."

Within the head of Festergrimm's robot, fused and connected to the cogs and levers inside, are pieces of bone.

Human bone.

Just like the legend says.

Lord Kraken, when he had the robot rebuilt, really did use parts of its original creator, too.

And as we look again into the golden eye lamps in the robot's face, it suddenly seems that we see more than just filaments inside. Something else is in there—something familiar and human.

"Mr. Ludo?" Violet whispers.

A tear falls from her eye and slides around the edge of one of the lamps. She reaches down and lays her hand on the robot's head. I do the same.

Pang, goes one of the bells in its mouth, softly, with a dull chime.

Dong, goes another. The bells are cracked.

Rang.

"Pandora," I say, nodding down at the bronze face and adding a tear or two of my own. "Yes. Yes, Pandora. I promise . . ."

"Herbie?" says Violet, looking at me in confusion. "Herbie, what . . . ?"

"I *promise*," I say again to the Mr. Ludo I can see in the robot's eyes, "that I, Herbert Lemon—Lost-and-Founder at the Grand Nautilus Hotel—will find Pandora and bring her safely back home."

The eye lamps flare bright again in brief acknowledgment.

Then, with a sudden crash that echoes horribly in this cavernous place, the mighty spring that drives the robot finally slips its housing and explodes out through the bronze plates of its torso. Clockwork parts scatter and clatter in the void. The robot's second arm loses power, and with it his grip on the ledge. The metal giant falls away, tumbling down into darkness, his eye lamps winking out.

There is a long, long silence until, from somewhere dizzyingly far below, comes the echoing boom of mechanical oblivion as Festergrimm hits the invisible bottom and shatters into a thousand pieces.

"Herbie . . ." Violet sits back on the ledge. Even in the utter dark that remains, I can tell she is staring at me in horror. "Herbie, what have you done? How can you ever promise such a thing?"

I know what Violet is thinking. I know how impossible it must seem that I can Lost-and-Founder my way out of this one, not after centuries have passed and the girl must be nothing but bones and dust by now. And yet . . .

"I said it," I reply, quietly, "because I meant it."

Because, I tell myself, somehow I just know that the fate of little Pandora, lost in the Netherways so many years ago, is tied to that of my own, found washed up on the beach in Eerie-on-Sea. Even if it'll take a whole new adventure, and all the luck and bravery in the world, to find out why.

But I don't yet know how to explain all this to Violet.

"Now what?" says Vi, after a long silence.

We are still sitting on the ledge, in the dark. If we hoped our eyes would get used to the tiny light that comes down from the hole in the street above, we are disappointed. We can see nothing.

"What I wouldn't give for my basket of lost flashlights right now," I say. "All I know is there is a breeze, from over there."

"Over where?" Violet asks. "I can't even see where you're pointing!"

"In the legend," I reply, "Pandora said she could sense a passageway, and she set off to explore. I reckon that passage is where this breeze is coming from. And though I hate to say it, I also reckon we have no choice but to try it ourselves."

"Even though nobody ever saw Pandora Festergrimm alive again?" says Vi.

I shrug, but Violet can't see that, either.

So, I get to my feet. Then, holding out my hands to feel for the rock wall I hope is there, I start edging my way toward the unknown.

"Herbie, this is madness," Violet whispers behind me, a note of despair in her voice I've never heard before. "Herbie, come back!"

But I'm so scared, I cannot speak.

Until, suddenly, there's a noise. A noise that fills me with hope again.

"Can . . ." I manage to get out, "can you hear that?"

"Yes!" Violet cries. "It sounds like . . ."

"Purring!" we say together.

From all around, echoing within the invisible cavern, there comes the steady rhythm of a rumbly purr.

We look up, and there—far, far above us—in silhouette against the light from the hole in the street, is the unmistakable shape of Erwin the bookshop cat, peering down.

"Me-ow?" he asks, matter-of-factly.

"Yes!" Violet calls up. "Yes, we're OK! We're here!"

"We-ow!"

Then another shape appears, and another and another.

"Violet!" cries the voice of Jenny Hanniver. "Herbie! Oh, thank goodness!"

"Golly!" says the wobbly voice of Mrs. Fossil. "Is it really them?"

"Hold on," booms Dr. Thalassi. Then, his voice less echoey as he calls to others on the surface: "Bring ropes! Send for the fisherfolk to bring ropes! They're still alive!"

CHAPTER 43

THE KING OF EERIE-ON-SEA

Have you ever climbed up a rope ladder when it's dangling in a void, and when every step sends it swinging? Well, if you have and you didn't squeak, then you are braver than me! But I'm just grateful for any way to get back up to the surface and the battered streets of Eerie-on-Sea.

"Almost there, Herbie," calls Dr. Thalassi, leaning into the hole and grabbing my hand. "Easy does it."

And then I'm out and trembling on the cobblestones as the doc reaches down for Violet, who was just behind.

"Oh, wonderful!" cries Mrs. Fossil, clutching her hands together.

Jenny gathers Violet up in a huge hug. I don't get a hug, but the doc gives me a slap on the back, which is almost as good. Except . . .

"Ow!" says Dr. Thalassi, pulling his hand away with a frown. "What on earth . . . ?"

Then he turns me around and says, "Herbie, what's *that* doing there?"

And he lifts something off my back, which comes away with a reluctant tug on my jacket. The doc holds it up so the streetlight can catch its pearly sheen.

"Clermit!" I gasp, seizing the shell in delight. "I thought I'd lost you!"

He must have detached himself from the rest of the robot and survived the fall. And then climbed back up to reach me! From inside the shell, the clockwork hermit crab extends one brass arm and snips his scissor pincers at me in greeting. Then he retracts the arm, ticks down to silence, and goes still in my hands.

I slip him under my Lost-and-Founder's cap, where I now know, once and for all, he truly belongs. Only to find the doc looking at me beneath his thunderous eyebrows.

"I thought I told you that device was immensely rare and valuable," he says. "I thought I told you to keep it safe!"

"I . . . um." I search for a suitable grin. "I can explain . . ."

But Dr. Thalassi sighs and holds up his hands in surrender.

"You are the Lost-and-Founder, Herbie," he says, though his eyebrows remain disapproving. "I said I was going to trust you with these things, and I will."

"What about Sebastian Eels?" says Violet. "Surely you can see now we can't trust him with anything. Ever!"

"Oh, he's the hero of the hour," says Jenny, making a sour face. "I don't think it matters what we think."

⚙🔘✿

It's a short time later, and we are all in Dr. Thalassi's office. The doc insisted on checking us over, after all that had happened. I ache from top to bottom, and Violet's cheek is bleeding again, but Vi and I have no patience with being fussed over.

"How can he be a hero?" Violet demands. *"Eels!"*

"Well, that's what the fisherfolk think, at any rate," Jenny explains. "He vanquished Festergrimm single-handedly and saved the town, or so they say. Apparently, people saw it happen."

"I don't know what I saw," Mrs. Fossil says. "There was so much smoke and brick dust!"

"But it was all his *fault*!" Violet is outraged. "*He* was to blame!"

"I'm sure," says the doc, "but the story of how he stopped some kind of out-of-control machine that was damaging people's property is already washing round the town like a freak tide. Whatever it was—and I never got a clear look myself—people say it was a metal monster."

"There wouldn't have been a monster at all," says Violet, "if Eels hadn't returned to Eerie-on-Sea."

"Whatever the truth of it," Jenny Hanniver replies, "he was carried in triumph on the shoulders of the fisherfolk back to his house, which he entered like a long-lost king returning to his castle. They say that in his hands he held something bright and silver, which seemed to cause him great delight, though I expect we'll never know what *that* was."

And she turns a look of inquiry on to us.

Violet opens her mouth to speak, but I give her a nudge. She closes it again. Once more I realize that we know a great deal more about what's been happening than these three adults who watch out for us. But I don't know how to begin to explain it all, or even if they'd believe us if we did.

"Normally," I say instead, "at the end of an adventure, there's cake. And hot chocolate. And I don't see why this one should be any different."

"I'll put the kettle on," Mrs. Fossil says, as she bustles off to the doc's kitchen, while the man himself packs up his medical bag. Jenny gazes thoughtfully through the window and out over the town, where the last fires are finally being brought under control, and the voices of the townsfolk can be heard as they begin to count the cost of this destructive night.

"I think there might be some dry fruitcake in the bread bin," Dr. Thalassi calls after the departing beachcomber.

My heart sinks. *Dry* fruitcake?

"I'll just clear a space," the doc adds. "Herbie, Violet, perhaps you could help me?"

And so, between us, we carefully gather up the papers and charts that cover the doc's desk and put them into a nearby wooden box.

"What are these things?" Violet asks, seeing how old the documents are.

"Ludovic Festergrimm's private papers," says the doc. "Or what remains of them. They have been in storage in the museum for years. I thought I'd give them a glance over, what with all the recent interest in the waxworks gallery. I wondered about putting together a small exhibition in the museum, but I doubt Eerie-on-Sea is in the mood to hear the name Festergrimm again in a hurry."

"These were written by Mr. Ludo?" Violet says, staring down at the papers in her hand.

"They were," the doc replies. "Those pages you have there are from one of his notebooks. They were recovered after his death. As you can see, he wrote a lot about his daughter, right from the moment she was found."

"Wait," I gasp, "she was *found?*"

"That's what I said," replies the doc.

"But I thought the whole point of the legend was that she was never found!" I say. "She's Pandora Lost, not Pandora Turned-Up-Again!"

"She *was* lost, Herbie," replies the doc, "in the end. She fell down into the Netherways, never to be seen again. But I'm talking about at the *start*, when Ludovic Festergrimm—Mr. Ludo, if you prefer—discovered her in the first place, years before, on his first ever trip to Eerie-on-Sea."

I slump onto a chair. I think, after everything else, that this unexpected twist might just cause my brain to actually explode.

"You need to explain, Doc," Violet says, sitting beside me, still clutching the papers in her hands. "Please."

"It's all there, in his own handwriting," the doc replies. "According to Mr. Ludo, the very first time he came to the Eerie Winter Fair, he was alone. While he was here, someone told him about mysterious tunnels and caves beneath the town, so he decided to visit them for himself. He was gone for a lot longer than anyone expected, and when he returned, he had a little girl with him. He said he found her, alone in the dark, and brought her back to the surface. He expected to find the girl's parents, desperately relieved to see her again, safe and well, but instead—"

"But instead *what?*" I blurt out.

"But instead, Herbie, there *were* no parents," Dr. Thalassi replies. "No one had ever seen the girl before. She was a complete stranger to everyone in Eerie-on-Sea."

Mrs. Fossil comes in then, with tea (no hot chocolate!) and the driest loaf of fruitcake I have ever seen in my life (boo!).

"But didn't the girl say where she was from?" Violet asks.

Dr. Thalassi shrugs.

"She couldn't say," he explains. "Or maybe she couldn't speak a language anyone could understand—it's not clear from the writing. In any event, Mr. Ludo ended up adopting her and naming her Pandora. After that he always brought her on his annual trips to Eerie, and probably elsewhere—dressed up as if she were made of clockwork herself, as part of the spectacle of the great Ludovic Festergrimm's Mechanical Marvels. It is a bit peculiar though."

"In what way?" asks Jenny, coming back over to join us.

"Well, Mr. Ludo's dates don't really add up," says the doc, taking a slice of fruitcake and dunking it in his tea. It looks so dry, I'm surprised it doesn't empty the cup in one go!

"When Mr. Ludo first found her," he continues, "the girl was described as being a child of about eight years old. But when she was lost, ten years later—after Mr. Ludo had apparently been bringing her with him to Eerie-on-Sea winter after winter—she was described by people who were there that day as still being about eight years old."

I look at Vi, unable to speak, only to find Vi is already looking back at me with wondering eyes.

"Oh, these old papers and things are always a bit muddled," says Mrs. Fossil, eyeing the fruitcake suspiciously. "Must be a mistake."

"Do you have any papers, Mrs. Fossil?" I ask. "That might make it clearer?"

"From your brilliant ancestor?" Violet adds. "Felix Fossil? He was a big part of this story, too, wasn't he? And someone you and your family must be really proud of."

"*Felix* Fossil?" says Dr. Thalassi, seemingly surprised that Mrs. Fossil has any noteworthy ancestors. "What's all this?"

And Violet quickly explains how the Fossil family's most notable member was a master of clockwork, too, in a way and the founder of Festergrimm's Eerie Waxworks, all those years ago.

"There are some old papers," Mrs. F admits cautiously, when Violet has finished. "And notebooks and things. And a really nice painting of Felix, too. I could show you, Doc. Maybe . . ." she adds, as if testing out the idea, "maybe you would like them for the museum?"

"Definitely!" says Dr. Thalassi, looking utterly amazed. "It sounds like I'll have enough material for an exhibition, after all."

⚙ ⬤ ✿

"More and more mystery," Violet whispers, leading Erwin and me into the main hall of the museum, so we can talk more privately. From back in the doc's study, we can still hear the reassuring buzz of adult conversation. "So, Pandora wasn't just *lost* under the town," Vi says, "she was *found* there, too! What does it all mean, Herbie?"

Well, I don't know what it all means, do I? And yet I still have that feeling, somewhere on the itchy bottom of my soul, that I do know more about Pandora and the Netherways—*and* the deepest secret of Eerie-on-Sea—if only I could remember it.

There is a sudden tapping on one of the museum's great Gothic windows. In a glass pane, a single yellow eye peers in at us, above a yellow beak. Then that beak taps the window again.

"Bagfoot!" gasps Violet. "You made us jump! But look," she adds, showing her empty hands, "I don't have anything for you."

"I do," I say, holding up the uneaten slice of dry fruitcake I've been carrying around politely for the last half an hour.

Violet opens the museum window, posts my piece of cake out to the waiting seagull, and snatches her hand back inside before she loses a finger.

"Eerie-on-Seagulls may be a ragtag lot," she says, tapping

her thanks to Bagfoot on the glass, "but I'm happy to have them on our side."

"Ffft!" goes Erwin, bristling all over and flattening his ears.

"Herbie," Violet asks, picking up the cat, "were you really ready to go off into the Netherways, in the dark, to search for lost Pandora?"

I flap my hands. I don't really know how to answer this, because yes, at the time I was. But now, after being rescued and brought back up to the light—*and* after what Dr. Thalassi has told us about the strange little girl from the legend—I really don't know what to think.

"We couldn't have just stayed sitting on that ledge forever, Vi," is all I can think to say, "could we?"

"Well, thank goodness for Erwin, then!" Violet replies, burying her face in the softness of the cat's fur while he purrs up a storm of contentment.

"So, what do we do now?" Vi continues, once she's come back up for air. "After everything we did, Eels still got the gyroscopic regulator. The only map of the Netherways ever made! That means the deepest secret of Eerie-on-Sea is his for the taking, Herbie, and we still don't even know what it is. He's won! Sebastian Eels has won!"

I straighten my Lost-and-Founder's cap and puff out my buttons.

"He may have the map," I concede, "but Eels hasn't won anything yet. Not while you and I are on to him, and Erwin, too, and Clermit's under my cap. No matter what Sebastian Eels does next, Violet Parma, we'll be there to stop him, or my name isn't Herbert Lemon (which it is). And that's all there is to it."

Does this sound brave? I hope it does. Because whatever happens next, whatever dark deeds our archenemy gets up to in the shadows beneath Eerie-on-Sea, one thing is clear: It really will be up to us to stop him.

Even if it turns out to be the greatest and most dangerous adventure of all.